APHOTIC

D.R. MATTOX

Copyright © 2020 by D.R. Mattox

ISBN: 978-1-7353023-5-5

Edited by: Sara Kelly

Published by WARREN Publishing
Charlotte, NC
www.warrenpublishing.net
Printed in the United States

To Lillie

TABLE OF CONTENTS

CHAPTER ONE
STONO

Shadows and light, through trees and clouds, fought to cover the road of the two-lane highway we traveled down. My dad was driving, my mother was in the front seat, and my little sister, Aileen, sat in the back with me. The feeling of yet another family trip to the beach was one of ease, like rereading a good book whose story and ending you know by heart.

It was hot and sticky outside, but the air inside felt cool as it passed slowly from the front vents to the back windshield. We were in an old SUV. The seats were cloth and black, and the interior of the frame was white, matching the exterior. The trim of the windows consisted of metal and chrome, with black rubber seals. Worn stickers from national parks and family favorite venues layered the back bumper.

My attention drifted between my phone and the window. I took in the drive and enjoyed the scenery, shifting my focus whenever I received a message alert. I'd unlock, scroll and read, rattle off a response, then look out the window again. One chain was a group text with some guys, good friends of mine, debating which sport was the best. Another thread was with a girl I was close with, truly as a friend and not more, but I found her messages more interesting than sports.

As we moved from highway to highway, the path stayed straight for long stretches. It was apparent the highway engineers saved every dollar by keeping the roads linear without curves. I appreciated this efficiency, though I longed for a curve or two so I could pass the time wondering what was around the bend. Lacking this entertainment between texts, I focused on the road itself.

First, I studied the pavement. As each highway passed over a county line, the pavement type would change. Some would be new, some old, some concrete, some asphalt. My favorite stretches consisted of old asphalt, which had lost its dark black hue and faded to light gray, almost like concrete. In addition to the fade, the old asphalt showed worn aggregate giving way to alligator cracks and tire ruts. Many cracks had been injected with blackish glue as a crude and simple fix. The edge of the road was lined continuously with brush and patches of bright sand, and I marveled at the presence of sand so far inland.

The pavement cracks and crops of sandy brush passed by as I tried to focus on the long white line. We forever chased its end as motion roared through the windows. Mile after mile revealed sawgrass, palm trees, and Spanish moss hanging low from snarly oaks. A pair of off-brand Jordan's hung from branches every now and then, accompanied randomly by Christmas ornaments. It was artistic and ghostly.

I listened as Aileen and my mother playfully argued about how the ornaments and shoes came to hang from the high branches. My mother was adamant that monkeys had been trained to put them there, while Aileen was not buying it. Aileen looked to my father, asking him to dispel the monkey theory. Instead he elaborated on it, further supporting our mother's claim. According to our father, not only were there hordes of monkeys in the area, decorating trees with Christmas ornaments and old pairs of shoes, but those same monkeys had escaped from an old facility on a haunted island where they had been used for testing and experiments.

Now desperate and less confident in what was true, Aileen looked to me, as her big brother, for help. Her face was uncertain and her eyes searched mine for any tells that could aid her. I gave her a quick wink and slightly shook my head no, careful to not let our parents see. Aileen responded with a grin, and silently mouthed, "Thank you" back in my direction. With confirmation from me that the story was a lie, she engaged once again with my mother and father, intent on convincing them their monkey theory was incorrect, and there had to be another explanation for how the ornaments and shoes ended up on the trees.

Enjoying Aileen's banter with my parents in the background, I turned my attention back to the road. Slowly moving down in elevation, we started to encounter marsh and tides, spanned by high arching bridges. A marshy smell started to seep through the vents.

I leaned my temple against the warm glass. The marsh was bare, showing low water lines and retreating inlets. The tide was low, and it appeared the water was still moving out. We were close to the coast now, maybe a few miles away. Farther up, along the bare marsh, appeared a small tree, petrified by salt water, with twisted branches and no leaves. The tree appeared to glisten, and as we came closer, I could see streamers and ornaments adorned its branches. Its shine matched that of the sad tree from "A Charlie Brown Christmas," freshly wrapped by Linus's blanket.

We came even with the Charlie Brown tree. For a second, there appeared to be the silhouette of a body standing behind the tree. As we passed, I strained to get a better look, but there was no one there. The tree's petrified branches and adorning streamers had created a shadow in the wind.

"We're almost there," said my father, his voice bringing me back.

The tree passed in a blur. I turned my attention to a sign nailed to faded wood posts.

WELCOME TO STONO BEACH

"Are you guys interested in some beach time? We've got some time before supper and the weather is decent," said my mother, with an opportunistic tone.

"Please, Ko, can we?" Aileen asked me.

"Sure," I replied.

"I'll drop you off at the pier while your mom and I get groceries and pick up the key for the house," said my father. His eyes shined with our destination in mind.

We crossed over the final bridge to the island. Stono Beach was a barrier island protecting the mainland from the Atlantic. The island was accessible via a single bridge spanning the last cloves of marshland. As visitors cleared the bridge, they were greeted with three immediate options, the approach being perpendicular to the ocean.

The first option, to the left, was a state park introduced by a humble welcome center and accompanied by a campground. The second option was the Stono Beach pier where the highway ended. The Stono Beach pier extended a short way into the Atlantic. It had a restaurant and beach shop, along with beach access parking.

The third option, to the right, included two roads providing three rows of beach houses: the first row was beach front; the second was the middle row, and the third row lined the marsh that separated Stono Island from the mainland, with houses and long skinny wooden docks providing boat access to the marsh inlets.

"What do you guys think about supper at seven? Pizza okay?" said my mother as she twisted in her seat to look at us. Falling into view with her turn was an old diamond necklace she wore. The chain of the necklace had faded, but the diamond remained beautiful. I couldn't remember a time when she didn't have the diamond around her neck. It was like a tattoo for her.

"Mmmmm … pizza. Are you okay with that, Ko?" said Aileen.

"Sure," I replied, giving the same answer as before.

"Okay, we'll pick you up here at seven. Please be in this same spot," my father said in an even tone we knew to take seriously.

We pulled into the beach access by the Stono Beach pier. Aileen and I hopped out, shut our doors, and watched as our parents pulled away. Facing the ocean, we started walking toward the State Park.

It was mid-afternoon, overcast, and not too hot with the ocean breeze. We walked past the park welcome center and opted to veer toward the campground, instead of the beach. The campground road was dirt and sand, winding below a thick canopy of live oaks draped with moss. Island brush and palms filled the space from oak to oak, offering little escape from the road. Branches and leaves at eye level were still, while the tops of the oaks swayed with the breeze, causing shadows to shift around us as we walked.

Aileen ran ahead, swinging a long necklace she had made. She loved crafting and often made what she considered to be necklaces, but they were much too long and could almost double as a jump rope for someone her size. Often, she would braid one of these necklaces into her hair, leaving one wavy strand of green, purple, or blue to interrupt her long blonde hair. Aileen was nine years old, six years my junior, and beautiful. It was obvious she would one day be a very pretty woman. However, her current beauty was less about appearance and more about her being. She was innocent, glowed with youth, and concerned herself only with the next adventure or game. Society had no hold on her yet, as it had nothing to offer that could garner the attention of her blue eyes.

We exited the thick canopy and entered a clearing where the campground began. There were three or four rows of campsites stretched before us, bound by marsh to the left and dunes to the right. The ocean was audible over the dunes as its waves continued their endless battery of earth.

We strolled through the grounds, admiring the various accommodations set up by strangers. The campground was full. There were tents, campers, and RVs. The more seasoned campers had extensive dining tents with bug-proof screens, makeshift awnings for rain, and impressive grilling stations. Aileen admired the sites where campers had strung lights across awnings, or between two trees. Most sites had basic white lights, which were pretty and created a nice atmosphere, while other sites employed a more bombastic combination of colored lights in different shapes. One camp had lights in the shape of large parrots, alternating between blue, yellow, green, and red, slowly blinking back and forth. These were Aileen's favorite.

"Look at the parrots, Ko! Aren't they silly?" said Aileen.

"Very silly," I squawked in my best talking parrot impersonation, which Aileen responded to with a giggle, leaning her head into my side as we strolled along.

We happened upon a large playground that was a dream for children. It sat in a clearing, away from the campsites, and was enclosed by a wall of oaks and hanging moss. Wooden guardrails had been placed intermittently in an attempt to designate the perimeter of the playground. Thick grass was randomly interrupted by splotches of sand. Two black jungle gyms stood in separate corners and near the perimeter. In the center of the clearing was a large network of gray wooden playhouses, that resembled a military fort. The houses were connected by swing bridges, rope ladders, monkey rings, slides, a row of swings, and various beams or poles—for use by the most daring of children in transferring themselves from one fort to another. The center of the fort network had a pinnacle, the throne, with a large steel spiral slide for transporting the king or queen from their perch back to earth.

"Aileen, it's like a castle. Do you want to be queen?"

"Up there?" Her eyes were wide as she tilted her head back to look.

"Yeah, the middle part could be the throne from which you rule. As far as your eye can see counts as your land and your people."

Her feet firmly planted on the ground next to me, she turned her head from side to side, taking inventory of the grounds. She scrunched up her face, saying, "I don't see very much."

"That's because you're down here. Go up there and tell me what you see." I gave her a nudge of encouragement.

Her eyes inquisitively narrowed, and her lips pursed as she approached the nearest rope ladder. She ascended, awkwardly, laughing as she almost fell at first. Conquering the first ascent, she approached a swing bridge. She leaned over the bridge and reached her arms to grab the rope railings, steadying the bridge before proceeding forward. She took her first step, keeping one foot planted, and the bridge shuddered. Pulling her lead foot back, she looked at me with a grin before launching herself across the bridge, allowing her momentum to carry her to safety before the swing bridge could think about shuddering again. From there she quickly climbed a ladder, taking her to the pinnacle. She reached her throne and looked back with an expression of being mildly entertained.

"I'm here. What am I queen of?" Aileen spoke loudly to cover the new distance.

"What do you see?" I asked, raising my voice as well.

"I see you."

"What about the campsites? You can see the lights through the trees."

"Does that count?"

"Yeah, you're queen of the campers. They have to do whatever you order."

She smiled, her voice moving to a loftier tone. "Hmm … I'll leave them alone for now … I'll get them later."

I moved closer to the base of her tower. "What else do you see?"

She surveyed her surroundings, returned to the side I was standing near, and, meeting my eyes, she shrugged and said, "I don't know."

"What do you mean, you don't know? Please, your majesty, look again."

Matching the lofty tone she had used previously, I elaborated on her kingdom as she looked on from her perch.

"Queen Aileen, the first of her name, we have established that you are queen of the campers through the trees. No small responsibility. Surely, over the dunes you can see the horizon of the ocean? This means you are royalty in the ocean's eyes, and it belongs to you along with everything in it. How vast the ocean is that you rule over! Furthermore, that ocean is connected to other oceans. Why the world has multiple oceans is beyond me, as they are all connected to one another. Truly they are one ocean, regardless of the foolish lines men have tried to draw between them. This makes you queen of all oceans, no matter how the world tries to split them up."

"Ko, what about the waves? I see the ocean, but the waves on the beach are hidden by the dunes."

"Your highness, the waves belong to the ocean. As we've established, the ocean belongs to you, meaning that what belongs to the ocean belongs to you. The waves are yours. Not just the ones we hear over the dunes, but the waves crashing in Ireland, in Japan, and even the ones which have frozen just before crashing into Antarctica."

Aileen was pleased. Leaning over the railing and closing her eyes, she let her feet dangle above the platform. She leaned back, setting her feet down again, and looking to her left, she eyed the marsh.

"What about the marsh? Am I queen of the marsh?"

"I'd say so."

"What about the fiddler crabs? Can I be queen of them?"

"Certainly. The fiddler crabs belong to the marsh, and the marsh belongs to you. If you ever doubt you're queen of the fiddler crabs, simply walk into the marsh. As you approach, the fiddler crabs will cover the ground by the thousands, causing the floor of the marsh to look like whitish blue mud. Once you come near, out of respect for the queen, they'll part and retreat to their holes in your honor."

"No, they won't!" she said with a laugh.

"Yes, they will. I promise."

Her face showed satisfaction with my promise, so I continued.

"Now that you're queen of the campers through the trees, the ocean, and the marsh, what will be your first decree?"

"What do you mean?"

"A new king or queen is expected to make decrees. The most beloved monarchs make decrees, which change things for the better. Think of the campers through the trees, the ocean, and the marsh, and a change that would make things better for everyone."

"I'm not sure." She paused. "What do you think?"

"I don't think I'm qualified to say. You're the queen, sitting high in your castle, and I'm a lowly subject down here in the slums on par with, or maybe lower than, the fiddler crabs. Should a fiddler crab have the power to suggest a decree to the queen?"

She tapped her finger on her chin and looked at the sky, recognizing the question as legitimate for someone in her newfound position. Allowing a few seconds of thought, she settled on her decision.

"You are a fiddler crab, and while I love the fiddler crabs, a fiddler crab should not be talking to a queen. It must be that you are appointed as a royal fiddler crab in order for me to hear you. Therefore, my first decree is that you are now a royal fiddler crab. Please, leave your mudhole and join me in the castle. But you can't come up to the throne; you have to stay lower than me in the castle."

A little caught off guard by her solution, but still enjoying the game, I approached the fort. I circled the network of structures, looking for the most grandiose of entrances. I settled on a fireman pole. I scaled the pole with ease but got stuck reaching my legs from the pole to the platform, struggling to shift my weight.

Aileen enjoyed the scene as I floundered for a few seconds before making it safely. Looking up at Aileen from my low perch in the fort, I continued.

"Your royal fiddler crab is here. I've abandoned my kind to be with you, my queen. What do you ask of me?"

Aileen reasserted the loftiness in her voice. "Honorable fiddler crab, what should be my first decree for the campers, the ocean, and the marsh?"

"You mean your second decree. Your first decree was appointing me to assist in making further decrees."

"Ahem, I mean, what should be my second decree?"

"Oh, brilliant and lovely queen, it is a great honor to have the privilege of being your council. As a lowly fiddler crab, spending my days digging in the mud and flashing my pinchers at the sun, I do not know all the ways of your kingdom. However, when the tide floods the marsh, with fish swimming above my kind, I hear tales of menaces that terrorize the ocean."

I paused, looked across the marsh, and shook my head as if too disturbed to continue. Aileen wore a rapt expression, her interest in the menaces growing with each second of my delay. With the intended effect in hand, I continued.

"These menaces are said to be fish themselves, but I do not believe it based on the stories I've heard. All the fish I know are cordial, speak little, and get along with most of the other fish, except for a disagreement here or there when fish food is scarce. The menaces I've heard stories of don't sound like the fish I know. It's said they're big, fast, mean, have razors for teeth, and instead of eating fish food … they actually prey and feed on other fish! It's horrible!"

"Do you mean sharks?"

"Yes, that's it! What chilling creatures we have terrorizing the waters. It seems unlikely, with sharks filling the ocean by the millions, that any other sea creature can live peacefully and happily, without concern that at any moment a shark might gobble him or her up. With that, my recommendation for the queen's second decree is to ban all sharks from the ocean. Imagine how much safer and more peaceful the ocean would be without sharks lurking both deep and in the shallows."

A seriousness settled in Aileen's face, with her lips pursing to indicate deep thought. "What have the sharks done to deserve being banned from the ocean?"

Aileen often shifted from free and playful to logical and empathetic, unwilling to judge. It appeared our latest banter may have triggered this shift once again.

"Imagine a family of fish going about their business one day, doing things that families of fish do, when out of the blue a shark appears and eats half the family, leaving the other half devastated and disoriented. Aren't you concerned for the remaining members of the fish family, who must live in fear and without their loved ones?"

"It makes me sad. But what does the shark have to do with it?"

"The shark is responsible for the devastation, is it not?"

"The shark is part of it, but I feel bad for the shark." Her voice quieted with pity as she spoke.

"So, you feel sad for the fish family, and also bad for the shark? That doesn't make sense. It seems to me that only one side of this scenario deserves pity, and that is the fish family."

"I feel bad for the shark because it doesn't know any better. When it eats the fish family, the decision is not the shark's, as the shark can't help how it was created. The shark is only doing what it was created to do."

"Then who is responsible?"

"I don't know," she said resolutely, her voice raising.

"If you could, would you change the shark, so it could live without having to hunt fish families?"

"That's not for me to decide."

Unable to recapture the playful side of Aileen's imagination, I decided our game had run its course. "Alright, your highness, we'll leave the sharks alone for now. Do you want to climb around a little more, or head to the beach?"

"Hmm, I'm going to climb a little more if that's okay?"

"Sure, I'll wait down there."

I climbed down, walked outward from the playground, and leaned myself against a fence post. I pulled out my phone and split my attention between it and watching Aileen as she started making her way from perch to perch, getting more creative with how she transported herself, whether using rope ladders, fireman poles, or climbing up slides.

My thoughts drifted as she played. What the remainder of the trip would be rolled through my mind: our family tradition of crabbing, night walks on the beach, and trading glances with pretty girls I wouldn't have the time or space to meet. Once home, I'd be back to enjoying summer with friends. I thought of the good times I was missing out on, being away, but I didn't mind it too much. Those good times weren't going anywhere, and I always enjoyed my time in Stono. I wondered how many more Stono beach trips I'd have with Aileen, and if we'd still do the trip once I was in college. It was strange to think of being gone and not seeing Aileen each day. Part of the prospect was exciting, the thought of college and being on my own, though more than anything I was hesitant to leave Aileen behind. I knew she'd be fine alone with my parents, but I couldn't shake a feeling of duty towards Aileen, as if she'd always need me by her side no matter her age.

I turned my attention back to the playground. By this time Aileen had conquered the grounds in most every way imaginable, so I interrupted her efforts.

"Hey, have you climbed enough? You ready for the beach?"

"Yeah!" she shouted in response.

She found the nearest slide and zipped down, her feet back on earth. We walked through a path cut in the dunes, turning left as we stepped on the beach. We walked until we reached the cay, looking for shark's teeth along the way.

The cay always offered the best selection of shells, and often the largest of shark's teeth. Far from the state park and rows of houses, we had the area to ourselves. Aileen and I stepped through the shells along the cay, with our hands behind our backs, often bending down to sort through "tricker" shells and hopefully pocket a shark's tooth. The tide was moving out as the afternoon lingered. This made the cay calm and inviting for a dip, though we were lacking our suits. Maybe later, during the week, we'd make the trek back to the cay.

"Ko!" Aileen's voice interrupted the sound of waves. She rushed toward me, her eyes fixated on a hand that was balled into a fist. "I found a big one!"

Aileen opened her hand, revealing a large shimmering black triangle. Her eyes watched mine in expectation as I examined her find.

"Wow." I started. I took the triangle in my hand and angled it back and forth, the light revealing different curves and shades of black and gray. It had many elements that made it look like a shark's tooth, but unfortunately it wasn't one. "This has to be one of the best tricker shells I've ever seen."

Aileen's face sunk in disappointment, expectation and hope turning to disbelief. "Aw, man, are you sure? How do you know?"

"Well, it can be hard to tell a tricker shell from the real thing, and I don't blame you for picking this one up. I would have picked it up as well." Each of us examined the black triangular shell in my hand. "It's the right size. I can see how the darker part looks like a shark's gum, while the other end is the right color of light gray to look like the tooth."

"But how do you know it's not a shark's tooth?"

I shrugged. "I'm just older and have seen a lot of tricker shells. Also, it feels too thin. A shark's tooth this big would feel thicker and more solid. Tricker shells always feel brittle."

"What does brittle mean?"

"It means it's easy to break." To demonstrate, I snapped the shell in half. "But don't worry about it. If you keep looking, you will find one."

Aileen accepted the fate of her tricker shell and, turning her focus back to the sand, continued her search. I checked the time. It was approaching six o'clock. It would take us an hour to walk from the cay back to the campground and then the Stono Beach pier.

I started us back. The ocean was now to our left and the tide was still inching out. Aileen walked ahead, her blue shirt fashioned into a tank top and her white capris rolled up high as she moved between the wet sand and the ever-changing ocean line snaking with the waves. I carried our sandals in one hand, with my shirt off and nylon shorts falling just above the knee. A light burn was settling on our skin, but nothing our summer seasoned bodies couldn't absorb over the coming days.

From time to time, I would pocket a shark's tooth and call Aileen back to examine it. One was reddish instead of black, which I explained to Aileen meant the shark's tooth was younger than the others we had been finding. I explained how all shark's teeth started off bleach white when they fell from a shark's mouth, and over thousands of years the teeth are fossilized and turn black before being swept on a beach for us to find.

"Have you ever found a white one?" said Aileen.

"I have not."

"What happens when sharks lose their teeth? How can they eat?"

"They have rows and rows of teeth. As they grow, they lose smaller teeth, and rows of bigger ones come front and center."

"That's like us," Aileen concluded with a smile.

"Sort of." I matched her expression with a smirk of my own.

We approached the campground again. Passing the campground and state park, we entered the last stretch of beach on our side of the pier and started angling up toward the parking lot.

It was a quarter to seven as we settled in, leaning against bollards, waiting for our parents. Cooling down, I pulled my shirt back on. We faced the mainland with the ocean behind us. The traffic entering the island was light as it approached from the same direction we had come from earlier in the day. Most vehicles opted for the rows of beach houses, while occasionally a camper would opt for the state park, eager to find a spot and settle in for the night.

Seven o'clock arrived and our parents had not shown up. It wasn't unusual for them to lose track of time. I checked my phone but found no missed calls or texts and decided to give our mother a call. There was no answer. I texted both my mother and father, and we waited. It was a little unusual for our parents to not respond, but it was not unheard of. We waited a little while longer. The island was but a few miles long, with our vacation house being roughly three quarters of the way down. It wouldn't take long for us to walk, so I texted our parents to let them know we were walking to the house via the beach.

Aileen and I started walking. The beach was wide now, with the tide at its lowest. The sun was sinking into western earth as dusk light rays slipped through gaps in the landscape and infringed on the corner of our eyes. What remained of the day's light was enough for scanning the sand in hopes of one last shark's tooth. Aileen had given up on finding a tooth and was content walking with her ankles in the remnants of a wave, her eyes scanning the ocean instead. The clouds of the afternoon had moved on, leaving behind a few high wisps soaking in a deep purple. This cleared the way for light beams to skip off the tops of waves, creating a layer of tiny flashes canvasing the ocean.

"Aileen, do you remember the story Dad used to tell about sea fairies?"

Still shuffling her feet through the water, she looked at me with a smile and nodded her head yes.

"So you remember that each time light hits the ocean, creating one of those tiny flashes, it's actually a sea fairy coming to the surface to grab light."

"Yea, but I don't remember how they're able to do it. Can you tell me the story again?"

"Sure," I said, and, taking a deep breath, I began to recount the story for Aileen.

"A long time ago, there were no sea fairies, just the flying kind. You see, fairies were born with the earth as shepherds of the earth. Specifically, they were charged with the nurture of trees, flowers, and crops, ensuring each species of plant thrived and made room for the next. Provided with supernatural wings, allowing them to travel great distances instantly, the fairies set to their work of developing and settling the wildernesses of Earth. With time, the earth's vegetation matured, and the work became easier. With their free time, the fairies invented dancing and spent their time jumping between tree branches, zooming through flowers, and occasionally playing pranks on slow developing humans. In time, some fairies became bored with flying through the woods and sleeping in trees. A small group of fairies abandoned the woods and began spending their time flying over the ocean and living in the dunes. Those fairies became known as dune fairies.

"In their days flying over the ocean, the dune fairies noticed the bottom of the ocean had patches of green. They were confused at first, but after many sunny days, and flying with their noses skimming the water, they discovered the floor of the ocean consisted of underwater forests. Very excited, they took this news to other fairies and explained how they believed fairies should start looking after the forests of the ocean as well. The other fairies laughed at them, saying it was impossible, too dangerous, and that fairies belonged in the sky.

"It wasn't that fairies couldn't be underwater due to a lack of air, as fairies don't breathe air, they breathe light. But in most places under the sea there wasn't enough light to sustain the fairies. During those days, fairies received the light they needed from the sun during the day, the stars and moon at night, and during cloudy nights or storms, the fairies would zoom above the clouds or to the other end of the earth to get the light they needed. However, if they went underwater, there was a risk the fairies could go too deep, where there's no light and it's hard to tell which way is up. If they didn't find their way back to the light in time, they could perish in the darkness of the ocean."

"Don't forget, Ko," Aileen chimed in, "about how the other fairies called the dune fairies names."

"That's right, the other fairies mocked the dune fairies, calling them "pollywogs" and "silly birds" for wanting to go underwater. Somewhat sad and feeling down, the dune fairies returned to their homes in the palm trees overlooking the ocean. Time passed, and the dune fairies continued to fly over the ocean, dreaming of exploring beneath its surface. One night, while lying on palm leaves and looking to the night sky, the dune fairies noticed a bright star. As they admired it, the star seemed to get brighter, flickering and flashing as it grew. The dune fairies had to shield their eyes as the light from the star, first slowly and then rapidly, filled their view of the night sky. The brightness reached its peak and at once subsided into a beam, which had tunneled down from the darkness of space and landed in front of them on the beach.

"The beam of light disappeared, leaving behind a boy standing in the sand. Shocked, the dune fairies slowly gained their wits and approached the boy. The dune fairies were amazed because, as they approached, it appeared the boy could see them, which was very strange because humans had never been able to see fairies before. The boy confirmed their suspicions and began talking with the fairies, explaining that he had been watching the dune fairies and wanted to help with their dilemma concerning the forests of the ocean.

"The dune fairies did not understand where the boy came from or how he could see them, but they proceeded to tell the boy how they longed to look after the forests of the ocean but could not due to danger of there not being enough light under the sea. The boy listened to their story and agreed the ocean could be a dark place and wasn't safe for fairies. Moved by the dune fairies, the boy revealed to them that he could communicate with Light, explaining that in his travels he had gained an intimate knowledge of Light and its ways, and he offered to share a secret to the dune fairies that would allow them to capture light and take it where ever they needed, even the bottom of the ocean."

Aileen jumped in again, "The secret from the boy had a catch though, at least that's what Dad use to call it, a catch."

"You are right again; the secret from the boy came with a price. If the dune fairies accepted the boy's knowledge regarding Light, and began tending to the forests of the ocean, the dune fairies would be required to reside underwater, forever, shepherding the forests of the ocean. The boy described how, if the fairies captured light and took it deep in the seas, the forests of the oceans would thrive. However, if after providing light to the depths, the fairies left the water and returned to the sky, the light they had submerged would follow them, leaving the newly developed aqueous forests to wither and die. The dune fairies were perplexed, as they discussed the boy's offer amongst themselves. They lamented how they loved dancing, flying above clouds, zooming through flowers, and how much they would miss those things. Many of the dune fairies countered by pointing out they could dance underwater, swim under currents, and cultivate submerged fields of ocean flowers to zoom through. Above all considerations, the curiosity and tendency toward adventure won out in the dune fairies, and they accepted the boy's offer.

"The boy taught the dune fairies the secret and illustrated how when light hit the ocean surface, there was an opportunity for a transaction between sky and sea. The secret made it so that the dune fairies would be able to live in the ocean, shoot to the surface of the sea, and capture light hitting the surface, taking it wherever they needed under the sea."

Aileen stared ahead with a smile as I neared the end of the story, her silence signaling I wasn't missing any important details.

"With the secret in hand, the dune fairies thanked the boy, wishing him well as they prepared to enter the ocean. The boy returned in kind and looked into the night sky. Same as before, a star began to shimmer and ever so slightly appeared a little bigger. With time, the star's light seemed to fill the night sky as the dune fairies shielded their eyes. Instantly, the brightness retreated, leaving behind a beaming tunnel of light connecting the beach to the cosmos. The boy stepped into the beam and disappeared, along with the light. The next morning, the dune fairies zoomed around the skies of Earth one last time, saying farewell to wildernesses they had known for so long, and the other fairies they'd be leaving behind. With a few last breaths of light in the sky, the dune fairies dove into the ocean and became what we know today as sea fairies.

"Now, each time a sea fairy zooms to the surface of the ocean to capture light, it results in an intense flash of light, which is what we see on the surface of the ocean to this day. We have the sea fairies to thank for the beautiful canvas of shimmering water we so often enjoy across the sea. Further, without the sea fairies, the Earth wouldn't have the beautiful corals of the Caribbean or the Great Barrier Reef of Australia. The forests and wildernesses of the ocean have thrived under the care of the sea fairies. They've even managed to invent new colors under the sea, which wouldn't have been possible on dry land."

With the story complete, I watched Aileen soak it in. A pondering smile spread across her face.

"That's a good story. I like it. If every time there's a twinkle on water it's a sea fairy, then there must be a lot of sea fairies," said Aileen.

"There are a lot of sea fairies, but you have to remember that they're lightning fast. One sea fairy can cause thousands of flashes of light across the world before the span of a second passes. That's why humans can't see them and have never widely accepted their existence."

Aileen was satisfied with my logic, as we returned to silently walking the beach.

We weren't far from the house. We had just enough light to navigate, ensuring each step landed on soft sand instead of a spiky shell. Aileen skipped ahead, chasing retreating waves to the ocean, as far as she could, before sprinting back, trying to outrun the next row of oncoming waves. She was fair to the waves, giving them an equal chance of catching her feet each time.

It was almost dark when we caught sight of the house, its roof barely visible past a few of the neighboring homes. Aileen was still walking ahead of me when she stopped, bent down, and picked something up. She slowly walked back my way.

"I think I found one, but it's probably just a tricker again," said Aileen.

"Let's see." I took Aileen's find from her hand and examined it in the darkness, turning the object to reflect as much light as possible from the moon, stars, and dusky sun. "Man, what a good find! It's definitely a shark's tooth. How the heck did you see this thing?"

Aileen's eyes widened as her mouth crept open. "Is it really one?"

"It really is. You've found your first shark's tooth. It's an extra special find considering the circumstances. Anybody can find one during the day, but you found your first one in the dark."

Aileen radiated as I handed her find back to her.

"Now be sure to hold on to that with both hands. If you drop it between here and the house, we won't be able to find it again."

Aileen obeyed and cupped the shark's tooth in one hand, placing her other hand as a sort of top to secure it. She walked behind me, with each step careful and calculated, as she focused her eyes on her hands to ensure nothing escaped. Our house came fully into view on the right, and we began to angle our way up the beach, away from the waves and towards the dunes.

CHAPTER TWO
A SCANT

Alone. Light poured in, but Joan couldn't feel it. Light and warmth hit her like a memory. Something she used to know and understand. The house was empty. They'd arrive soon. She paced. They would understand. They would help her. If they didn't, she would make them. Her brother was depending on her.

Joan pushed the thought of her brother from her mind. Outside she heard gravel under tires, followed by feet falling on steps. The footsteps reached the landing. They had arrived.

Simultaneous with the footsteps on the landing, she felt another arrival. Her breath shortened and her neck stiffened, her ears and eyes straining to confirm what she felt. Fear turned to dread, and dread to terror. She hid herself. Out of sight and her breathing low, she waited.

The front door of the house opened. A handsome man and attractive woman, both with dark hair and unusually blue eyes, entered. The man wore dark jeans with a light-colored shirt, while the woman sported a long, linen dress with faded, blue stripes. Closing the door, they turned and faced the main level of the house. Something unexpected greeted them. Joan followed their gaze across the room, where a strange figure now sat in what had been an empty chair a moment ago.

The strange figure was tall and lean with albino skin, short white-blond hair, and a white-blond beard covering a gaunt face, sunk by two craterous red eyes. Skeletally framed, the bleach white skin was taut and mostly hidden by a black suit, which covered a black vest, which covered a black shirt, topped with a black tie.

The source of Joan's dread wore a pleasant smile, directed at the man and woman standing at the home's entrance. The pleasant smile worn by the dark figure in the chair was a mask. Behind the mask was something sinister. The figure seemed to be a man, but he wasn't what he seemed. He had lost what made him human a long time ago. What remained was a convert, a being twisted and molded into a predator. A predator known as a Scant.

Neither the man, the woman, nor the Scant could see Joan. The shallowness of her breathing made her unsure of whether she was breathing at all. The man and woman were unmoved since stepping through the front door, their eyes focused intently on the Scant. Joan could tell from their expressions the man and woman were familiar with, and wary of, the intruder. The Scant broke the silence.

"There's a little girl whom I'd like to meet," said the Scant. Its voice was deep and hoarse.

The man and woman exchanged a glance, taking a step closer to one another.

"They're gone. Out of your reach," said the man sternly.

The pleasant smile of the Scant remained.

"I'm here. In the same space as you. I can feel the air move as you breathe. My presence is undeniable. Do you not see me? Why speak as if the inevitable can be avoided? Why speak as if I'm not here?" said the Scant.

It was the woman who responded this time, a trace of anger in her voice.

"Tell me, Scant, what do you see? I've always wondered, do you have sight? True sight? You speak of the inevitable, but which inevitable? I agree, the inevitable cannot be avoided. You are seen, and you are known, but only for a time. Your gaze is met by many, but where does the gaze of many return? Even now, your gaze is met by mine. Tell me, where does my gaze return? Does it land on anything?"

The Scant's pleasant smile faded as the woman spoke. Its dark red eyes were still.

"I am; I am often misunderstood. In the end, all understand. Your gaze lands close to where you think. You believe what you are seeing is nothing. You believe that I am passing through, with a beginning and an end to be observed. I am close to that. I am close to nothing. You'll soon learn the difference between nothing, and what I am."

"What do you believe you are?" said the woman.

The Scant remained perfectly still in the chair as it responded, though its voice tightened, causing the Scant's words to move a little faster, "They say there is nothing to be afraid of. I'm always close behind that thought, reminding them there is something to be afraid of. I am worse than black. I am worse than darkness. At least you can see darkness, know it. With me there is nothing to see or know, because there is no you when you are with me. There is no thought, no feeling, no love, no life, and no hope. I'm what you push out of your mind late at night, the truth you resolve to face another time, the truth you resolve to face after you've had more time, and after you've had life. It'd be a relief for you if I said I was death, but it's worse. I am nothingness."

The woman stood unmoved. The man put an arm around the woman's waist and pulled her close. The woman allowed the gesture to break her focus on the Scant, closing her eyes and leaning into the man as he embraced her. The man whispered to the woman. The words were quiet, too soft for Joan to pick up. Tears made their way from the shut eyes of the woman as she listened. When the hushed message finished, she lifted her head, a kiss completing their embrace. His left hand in her right, they faced the Scant.

The Scant's eyes lowered, drawn by a glow hovering above the floor between the man and woman. Looking closer, Joan could see that the glow was light, put off by a chain connecting the man's wrist to the woman's. The chain appeared to be small rings of light interlocking. The Scant's face shifted to amusement.

"Very well. You can go together. You won't last long where you're going, and when you fade and separate from one another, I'll be there to bury your light," said the Scant, rising from the chair.

"We'll see," the man said in an even tone. The chain of light joining their wrists seemed to vibrate as he spoke.

The Scant's eyes flickered with anger.

"I want you to know that what you are about to experience will be the fate of your children," the Scant said as it pulled a black cloth from its pocket. The Scant then let the black cloth fall, revealing a black Veil. Joan knew what came next. She had seen it once before, just a day or two ago in another place far away.

The Veil grew rapidly, extending from the Scant's outreached arm. Leaving the fingers of the Scant, the Veil hovered in the room, floating with a current in the space above their heads. "When I meet your children, I won't allow time for a chain of light to save them from being alone. I'll take one and then I'll take the other."

The Veil's movement seemed to react to the Scant's words, as if it were watching the Scant with anticipation. The Scant tilted its head back, as if looking beyond the ceiling, and closed its eyes. In response, the Veil froze above the man and woman, no longer flowing with the unseen current.

It was in that moment, with the Veil near and the Scant looking beyond, that the woman turned and looked in Joan's direction. She was hidden, unseeable, but the woman was looking her in the eye from across the room, as if the woman knew Joan was there. The woman slowly pulled off a necklace and set it down on the floor. The woman glanced at the necklace on the floor and then back in Joan's direction. There was no doubt now that the woman knew Joan was there, and the message was clear. The woman turned back to the man chained to her by light. They embraced, holding one another. Meanwhile, the Scant's dark red eyes returned from the beyond.

"Aphotic," commanded the Scant.

The Veil wasted no time, eager to hear the Scant's command. It descended on the man and the woman, expanding enough to wrap both completely. The shapes of their bodies were pressed against the fabric of the Veil. The contours of their bodies began to jerk and quiver as the Veil squeezed tighter. The silhouette of a man and woman embracing deformed into a shrinking amoeba.

Elevating their bodies and hovering above the floor, the Veil continued its digestion in silence while it slowly drifted toward the Scant. Amused, the Scant eyed the Veil as it floated closer. Still contorting, a now much smaller amoeba of bodies reached the

Scant. The Scant reached out, enclosing the black amoeba with both arms.

Pressing both hands inward, the Scant began to compress the remainder of the writhing blob. After a minute or so of squeezing, the Veil had returned to a flat piece of black cloth, lying limply in the Scant's hands. After neatly folding it, the Scant returned the Veil to its pocket, leaving just a corner of the black fabric hanging out. The Scant paused and glanced around the room.

Joan's heart stopped as the Scant's red eyes passed over her.

Seeing nothing, the Scant returned its gaze toward the ceiling, back to the beyond. Closing its eyes, the Scant began to whisper. The corner of the Veil responded and left the pocket once again. This time the Veil expanded slower and more gently. As it bled forth from the Scant's pocket, the black fabric began to wrap the Scant. The Scant calmly allowed itself to be engulfed by the Veil. Once encompassing the Scant, the Veil spun, shrinking until the space where the Scant had once stood was empty.

Joan was alone, again.

Allowing herself to breathe normally, she began to gasp. She wasn't sure if the gasping was from having held her breath, or if she was hyperventilating from fear. The gasping passed as she regained a shaky state of composure. The Scant's command, "Aphotic," still echoed in her mind. It was the second time she had heard it. First it was her brother, Leo, she had watched be taken by the Scant's Veil. Now, the man and woman she hoped could save her brother were gone.

Coming out of hiding, Joan slowly walked to the place where the woman had stood, and picked up the necklace from the floor. Holding it in her hands, she examined the piece of jewelry: its small copper chains put off a teal hue of oxidization. Lifting it up, the centerpiece fell, bringing into view a small diamond held in place by prongs with the same teal hue. She knew what it was, but not how to use it. It didn't matter now. The Scant would be back, and she needed to be ready. Concealing herself once again, she waited.

Time passed. She focused on the entrances to the house. Maybe they'd arrive before the Scant returned, and she could save them. Maybe the Scant wouldn't return at all. It seemed foolish to hope. She struggled to concentrate. Exhaustion was setting in, and the Scant's voice was echoing in her thoughts, corrupting her focus.

Aphotic. He's gone. *Aphotic.* They're gone. *Aphotic.* He's crushed. *Aphotic.* They're crushed. *Aphotic.* He's broken. *Aphotic.* They're broken.

The Scant's voice and images of the Veil's consumption looped in her mind. Her thought loop was interrupted by what was now a familiar feeling. Joan wasn't sure how much time had passed, but the feeling confirmed it was foolish to have hoped the Scant wouldn't return.

A small black void appeared in the room, instantly expanding and disappearing, leaving the Scant standing where it had stood earlier. The Scant seemed agitated as it settled in the same chair as before, but then calmed into a state of patience as it waited for the children to arrive. She matched the Scant's patience, remaining unmoved and taking shallow breaths, not risking any chance of giving herself away.

Light faded from the day. Dusk approached. The Scant, unaware of its unseen companion, seemed to have nervous tics. She flinched a little each time the Scant jerked. Maybe the involuntary movements were from anticipation of its prey's arrival, maybe the tics were from a past encounter, or maybe the tics were prompted by the last rays of light pouring in from the day. Joan liked to think it was the light causing the Scant's discomfort. The thought brought reprieve from the dread surrounding the Scant. The reprieve allowed for a new thought to form.

It had only been a couple of days since the Scant had taken her brother. When it happened, and she came face to face with the Scant for the first time, she froze. It wasn't just her fear of the Veil, it was something more. It seemed the Scant's gaze, once set, meant certain end for whomever it had fallen on. The man and the woman knew it. Once meeting the Scant's gaze, they embraced their fate, with no attempt to escape.

The only attempt at anything the man or woman made was when the woman looked at Joan and dropped the necklace on the floor. The woman picked that moment, as the Scant seemed to be looking elsewhere. *Looking elsewhere*, thought Joan, maybe that was it!

The moment before commanding, *Aphotic*, the Scant's gaze had turned upward, looking into the beyond. Could this be the moment, an opening in the Scant's grasp, to sneak past? She couldn't be sure, but she had to try. She had to be fast if she was to beat the Scant's Veil. Joan's thoughts were interrupted again.

The Scant had stood from the chair and walked toward the back of the house. It peered out the window that faced the beach. The Scant's steps had purpose as it returned to the middle of the room, giving away that the Scant had seen something.

It was nearly dark outside. The Scant switched on a lamp, turned the same chair to face the back entrance, and took a seat. For the second time that day, Joan hid quietly as the sound of feet falling on stairs grew louder. This time the guests and their steps climbed a separate set of stairs leading from the ocean. Joan's mind raced. She thought of trying to get to them before they entered but decided against it. The Scant had already set its gaze upon them, and if she moved now, all three of them would be consumed by the Veil.

The handle turned, and the door swung open. A young girl walked in, followed by an older boy. The girl was beautiful. She had been looking down at her hands, carefully minding her steps from the landing. The boy was handsome and looked to be a few years older. He was average height and lean, with shaggy brown hair and blue eyes. His long eyelashes accentuated sharp cheek bones. He wore black shorts and a loose white knit T-shirt embroidered with a swoosh. The girl wore a similar swoosh T-shirt, except it was blue. The boy closed the door and turned as the young girl called out, "Mom! Dad! You won't believe what … "

The girl stopped mid-sentence, her words trailing off. "Ko … "

"It's okay, Aileen." Ko pulled her behind him as he addressed the dark figure sitting in front of them.

"Who are you?"

The Scant responded hoarsely, "A friend."

"Where are our parents?" said Ko.

"They're gone," said the Scant before standing and pulling the Veil out once more.

"Where did they go?" said Ko, his voice growing tighter.

"I made a promise to your parents that I would take care of you. You'll be with them soon enough," said the Scant.

The Scant released the Veil. Like before, it expanded and seemed to float with an unseeable current. Ko stood frozen as his eyes followed the black fabric of the Veil, bewildered at what he was seeing. He absently reached for his phone, but it slipped from his hands and to the floor. Aileen wrapped her arms around her brother and buried her face in his side, keeping one eye on the Veil.

"Ko. I'm scared," said Aileen.

Ko looked down at his sister and then back to the Veil. Ko's expression of bewilderment was replaced by fear as he sought to shield his sister.

"It's going to be okay," said Ko.

The hint of a smile turned the corner of the Scant's lips. Just as eager, the Veil hovered above Ko and Aileen. The Veil didn't have eyes, but it seemed to be looking back and forth from the Scant to its prey. The Scant's eyes disappeared behind their lids, and its head tilted back.

Joan's moment had come.

She removed her obscure, revealing herself. She warped, pairing her moment with the moment of Ko and Aileen, and stepped from her moment to theirs. It wasn't like walking across the room to them but instead had the effect of instantly disappearing from one spot and appearing in another.

She grabbed the wrist of each and warped once more, pairing that moment with the same moment of a place far away, and stepped through.

Joan didn't waste time looking at the Scant or the Veil. The last she felt or heard from that last moment at Stono was an ear-splitting scream released by the Scant. Piercing through time, the echo of the scream stayed with her in the warp away from Stono. It was full of anguish and longing. Joan hoped never to hear anything like it again.

CHAPTER THREE
JOAN

Aileen lay near Ko, curled up and quiet in tall grass. The grass stretched out as far as it could, before disappearing under magnificent trees, which paled in height when compared to the purple granite mountains that looked down upon them. The sun was warm and the air cool as the breeze bent the grass around the siblings.

It was difficult for Ko to appreciate the beauty of the landscape due to an overwhelming motion sickness consuming his insides. He slowly climbed to his feet, feeling better as he gained his footing. It was a mistake, and misleading. The sickness returned, and he fell to the ground on all fours, throwing up what little remained in his stomach. Once relieved, Ko crawled away and found a new patch of grass to lay in. While on his back, he looked up at a blue sky with few clouds.

A shadow moved into Ko's view. Straining his head backwards, he was met by a girl looking down at him. She looked to be Ko's age, maybe a touch older. Raven hair streamed down each side of her gaunt face. She wore loose jean overalls with the legs tucked into brown hiking boots. The hollowness of her face and angularity of her shoulders, outlined beneath her snug T-shirt, revealed a petite figure within the baggy overalls. Her left eye was a piercing blue, and her right eye was half red and half emerald green.

"Are you okay?" said the girl, addressing Ko, who lay on the ground before her.

"I think so," said Ko.

"You'll feel better soon. It can be a little jarring," said the girl.

Stono, the beach house, and the Scant flashed in Ko's mind. Sitting up and regaining his wits, Ko faced the girl. Ko's senses were flooded with a panic, which bore itself out in a series of questions.

"Who are you?" said Ko.

"I'm Joan. Who are you?"

"I'm Ko."

"And her?" said Joan, motioning to Aileen, curled up in the grass nearby.

"That's Aileen, my sister. Where are we?" said Ko, slowly turning his head to survey the surrounding mountains.

"We're in a canyon of sorts, a long way from Stono Beach," said Joan.

Ko stared at Joan in disbelief. His uncertainty pushed his voice lower.

"What canyon is this? What state are we in? Wait, did we jump continents?"

"It doesn't matter," said Joan. "We're safe."

"Safe from what?"

"The Scant."

"I don't understand. You're saying that was real, at the house in Stono? The man and his possessed blanket?" said Ko.

"It wasn't a man. It was a Scant, and it wasn't a blanket. It was the Scant's Veil," said Joan.

Ko started to feel sick again. Not from motion sickness this time, but from facing a reality that should have been impossible. He paused to let the feeling pass, before continuing with questions to which he wasn't sure he wanted to know the answers.

"Joan, is it? How long has it been since we were in Stono?" said Ko.

"Twenty minutes or so," said Joan.

There was a patience in Joan's answers. She was intentionally being short and even with Ko, allowing Ko time to process small truths. This last truth was not small. They had traveled from the Atlantic Ocean to a mountain range thousands of miles away in a matter of seconds. Ko knew what had happened and that Joan had done it, but his imagination failed in offering an explanation as to how Joan had done it.

"How did you do it? You know, get us here?" said Ko.

"It's difficult to explain," said Joan, who hesitated and shifted her weight from one leg to the other, looking at their surroundings before returning her attention back to Ko. "There are different ways of describing it, but the simplest for now is that I can bend time. I can bend it in a way that allows me to take the same moment, from two different places, and sort of connect them, allowing me to move between the same moment in those two different places. It's called warping."

Ko released an involuntary laugh. It was a defense mechanism to allow space for processing. The weight of what had happened, what was still happening, continued to settle on Ko, and he was doing his best to bear the weight of their circumstances as Joan provided them.

"Okay. No big deal. We've just warped across time and space. I think I'm okay with that, but let me ask you something along those lines. When you grabbed our arms in Stono, there were flashes of other places, different from where we are now. I saw cities, an island, and even mountains which didn't look like these. Were those places real too?" said Ko.

"Yes. I had to cover our tracks to ensure the Scant couldn't follow us," said Joan.

"So, you're saying we went from Stono Beach, traveled all over the world, then arrived here, all in a matter of minutes?" said Ko.

"Yes," said Joan.

"I guess that explains why my stomach is now part of this beautiful landscape," said Ko.

Ko let the joke stand for a second. Joan gave no reaction, standing with her arms hooked behind her back and blankly looking down at Ko, who still sat on the ground. He took his failure at humor as an opportunity to try standing again.

Slowly shifting to all fours, Ko lifted his right foot, allowing it to plant, before pressing his weight on his right knee and pushing himself up. On his feet again, he took a deep breath and turned his attention back to Joan. Now standing a little taller than Joan, he continued his inquisition. Mindful of Aileen resting nearby, Ko lowered his voice.

"Joan, what did the man, you called it a Scant, want?"

Joan looked at Aileen. Joan's stoic expression twisted with a hint of concern. She took a step closer to Ko and whispered, "The Scant wanted your sister."

"What? Why?" said Ko.

"I think your sister is like my brother. I think she's a Celestial," said Joan, still looking at Aileen.

Joan appeared caught off guard by her own words and then seemed oblivious of Ko standing beside her, as she focused on Aileen, perhaps thinking of her brother.

Recognizing the pause, Ko allowed Joan a few seconds to think before interrupting with the next obvious question.

"What's a Celestial? Joan, I need more! None of this makes sense, and I need to understand what's happening. Please, if Aileen is in danger, I need to know everything."

Joan returned from her ponder, the concern in her face fading to a slight acknowledgement of Ko's worry.

"Very well. I think your sister is a Celestial. It's not something I fully understand, but if she really is a Celestial, then she's connected to light in a supernatural way. It's as if she and light can communicate. Her connection to light is why the Scant is after her. I don't know where Scants come from, or what they do with Celestials if they catch them. I just know that Scants are real, Celestials are real, and Scants hunt Celestials," said Joan.

"What do you mean, Aileen's connected to light?" said Ko.

"I told you. I don't understand it, so I can't explain that part to you," said Joan.

"Okay. Well, what about you? Are you a Celestial?" said Ko.

"No, I'm not a Celestial. I'm something else. Like you," said Joan.

"Like me? What do you mean?" said Ko.

"I'm what's called an Arc. If your sister is a Celestial, then you're an Arc as well. Each Celestial is born with an older sibling who's given the ability to bend time as a means of protecting their Celestial sibling from Scants," said Joan.

Ko struggled to grasp what Joan was telling him. Absent of being able to wake himself up from a dream, Ko had to believe what the strange girl, whom he now knew to be Joan, was telling him. He had to accept that there were beings he had never known about: Celestials, Arcs, and Scants. More than discovering and accepting the existence of these strange beings, Ko had to process that both he and his sister were now part of a new reality, or at least had always been part of it but had not known until now.

"So, we're not human?" said Ko.

"You're still a human. You're just also something else," said Joan.

"Okay, so I'm an Arc, like you. Can I do what you can do?" said Ko.

Joan allowed the slightest of smiles. "Not exactly. If everything I'm saying is true, and your sister is what I think she is, then you might be able to do what I can, but it would take some practice."

Ko wondered if his parents had known about Celestials and Arcs, talking with light, and bending time. If they did, why didn't they tell him? The events in Stono pushed their way to the front of his wondering thoughts. The Scant's words regarding his parents resurfaced in his mind: "They're gone." A sense of panic returned to Ko.

"Joan, where are my parents?"

Joan looked at the ground as she spoke. "They're gone."

Joan's words were the same as the Scant's. To Ko, the meaning behind her words felt like the Scant's as well. Each carried a sense of finality.

Ko's heart didn't sink. In a strange way, he had understood the fate of his parents at the first sight of the Scant and it's Veil in Stono.

"Are they dead?" said Ko, his voice soft.

Joan's gaze rose from the ground and met Ko's. "I'm sorry, but I don't know. I was there when the Scant took them. I'm not sure exactly where it took them or if they're still alive."

Ko didn't pry further. He knew the details would be cruel to learn, and cruel for Joan to relive. Instead, his mind tried to recreate the scene. Ko imagined his parents standing silently, facing the Scant. He didn't allow his parents or the Scant to speak in his daydream. They stayed silent in his vision.

Ko visualized the Scant's Veil being released and hovering above his parents, the same way it had hovered above him and Aileen. It was here that Ko's imagination was left wanting. He couldn't see what happened next. Joan had kept that part from him by intervening on his and Aileen's behalf.

Ko's imagination allowed him to step into the Stono house, the scene frozen while he moved freely through the room. He took a step toward his parents, reaching out to touch them and to tell them it was okay. His eyes moved between the Veil and his parents as he drew closer to them. The frozen Veil moved, twitching as if to look at Ko.

Ko shuddered and pulled himself from the daydream, turning his focus to Aileen, who was still lying nearby in the tall grass. He became filled with gratitude as he realized what Joan had done for him and Aileen, saving them from the Scant's Veil.

"Joan. Thank you."

The simple expression of indebtedness was all Ko could offer Joan, as no elaboration of words could represent the gratitude he felt.

"No worries," said Joan.

Ko's mind moved from gratitude back to introspection.

"I mean, how fortunate that you were there? We would have been goners if it weren't for you," said Ko.

Then it hit Ko: he didn't know why Joan was at the house in Stono to begin with. Ko's focus intensified. He began sizing up the tomboy standing in front of him. Joan's figure gave way to a baggy silhouette of overalls against the backdrop of mountains. It dawned on Ko that in their short time together, he had begun to trust the strange girl standing in front of him, but he didn't know anything about her. Ko realized that Joan may be the scariest unknown yet.

"Joan, why were you there, in the house at Stono?" said Ko.

☀ ☀ ☀

An edge returned to Joan in response to Ko's inquiry. She had been waiting for this. She had patiently waited for the boy, whom she now knew to be Ko, to process his circumstance and arrive at the question she needed him to ask more than any other. It signaled he had accepted his new reality, the fate of his parents, and the danger facing him and his sister—the Scant. It also gave Joan a chance to set the stage for what needed to happen next.

"Come with me and I'll explain," said Joan.

She motioned for Ko to follow her as she started walking toward a nearby outcrop of boulders. Ko appeared hesitant.

"Okay, but give me a second," said Ko.

He walked over to his sister and then knelt so he could whisper in her ear. Joan was unable to hear what Ko said and unable to see Aileen's wordless acknowledgement to what her brother had told her. Ko stood, seemingly satisfied with his sister's response, and returned to follow Joan.

They walked across the field and reached the crop of boulders Joan had picked out. They climbed the largest boulder and stood, looking across the field they had left behind, keeping Aileen in sight. From the vantage point of the boulders, the rolling grass looked more like a meadow than a field, nestled among the rocky landscape. The area was secluded, beautiful, and untouched. Ko didn't know it, but Joan had been there many times before.

"Ko, there are so many things I need to tell you. Much of which will explain why I was at the house in Stono. I expect you'll have questions along the way, but I think it's best if you let me finish before asking any questions. Can you handle that?" said Joan.

"I'll try," said Ko.

Joan took a seat on the boulder.

Ko took a seat as well and oriented himself to face Joan while still being able to keep an eye on Aileen. Ko appeared focused. To Joan, he seemed to assume the posture of judge and jury, intent to learn more about Joan, her motives, and why she was at the house in Stono.

Taking a deep breath, Joan began.

"I told you that each Celestial has an older sibling who's an Arc. As Aileen's older brother, you are her Arc. Same as you, I have—or had—a younger sibling who's a Celestial. My brother is close to Aileen's age. His name is Leo, and he was taken from me recently. Ultimately, that's why I was in the house at Stono, but before I get to that, I need to go back further so you know our story; that is, Leo's and my story.

"When Leo and I were very young, our parents left us in the care of a woman who was a friend of theirs. My parents told me to trust the woman, look after Leo, and that they'd be back for us soon. We waited, but our parents never returned.

"The woman we had been left with kept us and became our caregiver. It's odd, but she never gave us her name, nor did she tell us what became of our parents. Even odder, the woman taught us to call her "Stranger.""

"As we grew, Stranger began to teach Leo and me about Celestials. She explained how Celestials were beings connected with light, and that light was much more than it appeared. Apparently, all the light we see in the universe is bound together as a body of sorts, part of a greater being known as Light. I know, how to differentiate when speaking of light versus the being of Light? I still don't understand it myself. That aside, Stranger said that with age Celestials harnessed the ability to communicate with Light, and eventually gained the ability to become light themselves and move about the universe.

"While she taught us much, Stranger also sheltered us. We'd ask Stranger to tell us more about Light, or why Celestials existed, but she'd deflect and promise to tell us more when we were older. It was obvious she was hiding a great secret from us regarding Light and Celestials. Though, she did reveal to us that Celestials were paired with beings known as Arcs, who could bend and manipulate time as a means of protecting their Celestial siblings, until the Celestial could become light and move freely, out of reach from harm.

"Years passed with us under the care of Stranger. Eventually, though we had always suspected it, Stranger revealed that Leo was a Celestial and I was his Arc. It was at this time that Stranger also revealed the existence of other beings, besides Celestials and Arcs, named Scants. She explained that Scants were evil beings who sought to capture Celestials before they could grow with Light. She didn't explain why Scants sought Celestials, or what happened when a Scant caught a Celestial. She just told us Scants were nasty creatures who were to be avoided at all costs.

"Stranger herself was an Arc. Well before becoming our caregiver, her Celestial had grown and left her to follow Light somewhere in the universe. Anytime we asked when she had last seen her Celestial, she'd sidestep the question. For some reason, which we never figured out, Stranger always avoided talking about her Celestial. She was adept at avoiding even our most creative inquiries.

"In addition to teaching us about our true nature, Stranger taught me how to bend time. Stranger said that training normally didn't start for someone as young as me, but she insisted on it, citing it as a necessity for the safety of Leo. Stranger would start each lesson by saying, 'A being's capacity to act is limited only by that being's capacity for fear.' It was a saying I never understood, but Stranger made it ever present as I developed my influence on time.

"Leo developed in his own way as well. Stranger said it was difficult to know when a Celestial would mature, but Leo began to have moments where it seemed he wasn't with us. He began communicating with Light. It's not the same as you and I talking. For Leo, communicating with Light was a state of being, more of a physical feeling than language as we know it. Wherever Leo went, light seemed to gravitate to him. Though, it's not something you could see unless you were looking for it.

"We lived like this for years, with Stranger teaching and caring for us. We were a true family. We loved each other and wanted for nothing, though it didn't last forever. Our time together was interrupted.

"A few years ago, we were found. I don't know how, but a Scant appeared one day in our home. Stranger had never said what to do if we encountered a Scant. I don't think Stranger expected it would ever happen, but it did. When the Scant appeared, Stranger, without a word and before anything else could happen, grabbed the Scant and they disappeared. Stranger warped the Scant somewhere far.

"I took Stranger's act as a sacrifice, something to buy us time. So, I grabbed Leo and warped him away, fearful the Scant might return. I don't know for sure what happened between her and the Scant, but that was the last we saw of Stranger. Unfortunately, it wasn't the last we saw of the Scant."

Joan paused. It occurred to her that she had never talked with anybody about Stranger or Leo before. She had never known anyone else other than Stranger and Leo. Recounting her story for Ko was unsettling, putting words to memories for the first time. Joan's eyes drifted from Ko, who had been listening attentively, back across the meadow to where Aileen rested peacefully. How nice it would have been, she thought, to meet Ko and Aileen under different circumstances; perhaps Leo and Aileen could have been friends.

"Joan, are you okay?" asked Ko.

Joan turned her focus back to Ko.

"Yeah, I'm fine. Where was I?" said Joan.

"You were saying it was the last time you saw Stranger, but not the last time you saw the Scant," said Ko.

"That's right. Without Stranger, Leo and I managed on our own for a few years, always on the move, never staying in one place long for fear the Scant would find us. I continued honing the ability to bend time. The more places we went, the more locations I could warp us to, making us harder to find. Leo continued to mature as well, his connection with Light growing stronger every day.

"In our travels, Leo and I often helped ourselves to empty homes. If a property didn't have surveillance and I could see the interior, it was easy to warp ourselves inside the house. If anyone showed up, and we were seen, we'd warp somewhere far away, leaving the witness to wrestle with what they thought they saw.

"For the most part, we targeted the extravagant, usually crashing in mansions or yachts the wealthy would use on holiday. We developed quite a list of places we visited regularly around the world. One-percenters are really quite predictable. Most adhere to a cyclical travel schedule, spending the same parts of each year in the same parts of the world, alternating between long stretches of work or holiday. This made it easy for Leo and me to alternate between places, always timing our visits just after the owners had moved on to somewhere else. To keep from being too predictable, we'd do random excursions into the wildernesses of the world, camping for weeks in one hemisphere, away from civilization, before moving to another wilderness in the opposite hemisphere.

"Eventually, we felt safe again, happy, and thankful for what Stranger had done for us. After enough time had gone by, I thought we were in the clear. I figured our travel patterns must have been working or the Scant would have found us, or that Stranger had done something to neutralize the Scant for good.

"I was wrong. Which nearly brings us to the present, and closer to you understanding why I was in the house at Stono. It seems like a year ago, but it's only been a few days since Leo ... "

Joan paused again because she didn't know what to call it. She struggled to find the right words. And when she couldn't find them, she decided to just say it.

"It's only been a few days since Leo was taken by the Scant. We had been staying on a yacht docked in Australia, the owners none the wiser. We had spent a few weeks there and in New Zealand, and I decided it was time to move. I asked Leo where he wanted to go. He said he wanted to go to the mountains, specifically the Appalachians. I warped us to a small Appalachian valley we had been to before. We had gear hidden there from a previous stay, and we set it up, building a small camp. Same as other visits, after setup, I left Leo to go and get us some provisions. It didn't take but ten or fifteen minutes. I warped in a store during after hours, grabbed enough to last us a week, and warped back to our camp in the valley."

Joan paused once more. She felt a swell behind her eyes. Clenching her teeth and pursing her lips, she was determined to bury the tears inside of her. She couldn't allow herself sorrow. She could only allow strength. She turned from Ko, seeking to hide from him any pain or weakness.

Glancing across the field, her eyes followed the shadow of a cloud as it approached the base of a cliff. The shadow reached the cliff and started its ascent up the cliff face. The shadow cleared the cliff and eventually disappeared over the top of a mountain. The pressure behind her eyes disappeared as well. Back in control, she continued.

"I returned to the camp to find the Scant and his Veil hovering above Leo. At the same moment of my arrival, the Scant said, 'Aphotic' and released the Veil. I watched as the Veil descended upon Leo. I was motionless, without thought or action. All I felt was fear. As Leo disappeared under the Veil, I looked to the Scant and found its red eyes on me. I tried to move but couldn't. I tried to launch myself at the Scant, but something seemed to surround me, keeping me still. It was like a dream where you try to run but can't. It felt as if the Scant's eyes had a hold on me, but I don't think it was the Scant that stopped me from moving. It was something else, something inside of me.

"With Leo gone and its Veil back in hand, the Scant and I stared at each other for a while, each of us still. Finally, the Scant spoke. 'There's nothing you can do,' is what it said.

"Then the Scant released the Veil one more time, but not for me. Instead, the Veil descended on the Scant, and it departed. I was left alone.

"I don't know how long I stood there afterward. I was paralyzed, no longer by the Scant but by a desire to see my brother again and not knowing what to do next. Leo's eyes disappearing under the Veil have been all I can see since."

CHAPTER FOUR
QUANTUM

I t seemed obvious to Ko. The Scant's gaze had preyed on Joan's fear, holding her captive while she fought to act on behalf of her brother. Ko had felt the same sensation in Stono, but he didn't realize what it was at the time. It had been the eyes of the Scant, preying on Ko's fear of the Scant and its Veil. Somehow the Scant used its sight to access their fear and paralyze them.

A being's capacity to act is limited only by that being's capacity for fear. Stranger's saying, as recounted by Joan, echoed in Ko's mind. It had not registered with Joan, the significance of Stranger's words, but it registered with Ko.

Ko tried to tell Joan his theory. "Joan, when you faced the Scant and were unable to move, I think you were right about it being caused by something inside of you. I felt the same thing in Stono."

Ko's words brought Joan back. She had been silent, her mind seeming to have drifted somewhere else since sharing the details of her brother's abduction and her encounter with the Scant.

"Yeah, I'm fine. I told you I'd explain why I was in Stono. I promise I'll get there," said Joan.

Joan hadn't heard Ko. With her mind somewhere else, she had missed Ko's words and his attempt at delving into the power of the Scant's eyes. Ko resolved to let it go for now. While he felt his theory regarding the Scant's gaze was significant, he remained eager to hear the rest of Joan's story and how she arrived at the house in Stono.

"It's fine; take your time," said Ko, signaling for Joan to continue.

Joan reached inside her overalls and pulled out a small book. She ran her fingers across its brown tattered leather before opening it and fanning the thin pages across her thumb.

"It belonged to Stranger. After our first encounter with the Scant, when Stranger saved us, I grabbed it before leaving. It's full of notes from Stranger, symbols and drawings, which, for the most part, don't make any sense.

"After our second encounter with the Scant, this book is where I turned," said Joan as she raised the book with a light shake. "In the wake of Leo being taken from me, I combed every page, searching for anything that might show me how to save him. That's when I came across something I think you should see."

Joan flipped to a page she had marked and handed the open book to Ko.

"The first page is mostly nonsense," said Joan. "Scribbles and unfinished thoughts, but can you read what's in the bottom right-hand corner of that page?"

When Ko's eyes moved down the page, what he saw made him stop and stare, a look of puzzlement contorting his face. He looked up at Joan, then back down to the writing.

117 Valley Drive, Chatuge

"That's my address," said Ko.

"Odd, isn't it? I thought so too. It seems out of place with everything else in the book, but if you look closer, you'll see there's an arrow connecting your address to the following page."

Ko's eyes moved to the second page where the arrow continued before finishing next to Stranger's handwriting again.

Maris Family

"That's my name," said Ko.

"I know," said Joan.

Ko's eyes quickly scanned and consumed the rest of the page. Another arrow continued and connected Ko's family name farther down the page to what appeared to be a group of stars. Each star was a different shape, different magnitude, and flanked by its own short or long dashed accents. There didn't appear to be a way to connect the stars into anything significant. Like the arrow that led from Ko's family name to the star cluster, another arrow led from one of the stars in the cluster down to a phrase:

Portum Lux

"Ko, I know Stranger kept a lot from Leo and me to protect us, but she did mention Portum Lux every now and then. She described it as a haven for Celestials and Arcs, and she promised to take us there one day. She said the only way to Portum Lux was if you knew how to get there, or if you had a device called a Quantum. A Quantum provides a continuous path, or connection, between two places. Stranger knew how to get to Portum Lux, since she had been before, but for me, without Stranger or someone else who has been there, a Quantum device is the only other way to reach it."

Joan hesitated, allowing a few seconds for Ko to think. Ko's eyes were fixed on the pages, his eyes moving between his address and his family's name. He had already accepted that his parents had kept an entire world hidden from him, but seeing his family's name in Stranger's book, connecting his parents with Stranger, made his and Aileen's new reality seem more personal, knowing it had a history and contained relationships.

"What does it mean? How does my family fit into this?"

"Ko, I think the arrows connecting Portum Lux to your family name may be referencing your family as keepers of a Quantum—the device that could take me to Portum Lux, where I might find a way to save my brother. That's why I was in the house at Stono, to approach your parents and ask for the Quantum.

"After the Scant took Leo, it took me a day or so of looking through Stranger's book before finding your address. Once I got to your home in Chatuge, it appeared empty, so I entered your house to look around. I found a reservation that showed today as the first in a week-long stay at Stono Beach, as well as the address to your Stono house. From your home in Chatuge, I warped to Stono. When I got to the house in Stono, you and your family hadn't arrived yet, so I waited. When your parents arrived, somehow the Scant did too. I don't know how the Scant found you and your family, just like I don't know how the Scant kept finding me and Leo.

"I hid and watched as your parents faced the Scant and his Veil. I stayed hidden as the Scant waited for you and your sister to arrive, until the moment I grabbed you and brought you here."

Ko looked up from the book and focused again on Joan. He was satisfied with her story and why she was at the house in Stono. He resolved to wholly trust Joan moving forward. To signal this, Ko invited her to weigh in on something very important to him.

"Joan, do you think Aileen will be okay?"

Ko watched as Joan's face flickered a mixture of surprise and relief at his question. She appeared grateful to Ko for entrusting her and turned to look at Aileen before answering, "Yes, I think she will be okay."

Ko turned as well, and both he and Joan observed Aileen still peacefully lying in the meadow. Ko hadn't noticed it before, but the light of the sky seemed to be gravitating to Aileen, almost in a comforting embrace. He wondered if it was his imagination running wild with everything Joan had told him about Celestials and light. He glanced at Joan to see if she noticed it too. Joan caught Ko's glance, and gave a small nod, confirming that they were seeing the same thing.

A relief came over Ko, and his mind returned to the house in Stono. Now that he knew Joan's story, and how their paths had come to cross, other unknowns came to the forefront of his thoughts.

"Joan, when you appeared in the house, it was as if you truly appeared in the middle of the room. It's not like you were hiding in a closet or under the bed and then came out. How did you do that?"

Ko watched as his question pulled her attention from Aileen and back to him. He could see a spark in Joan's eyes. She seemed to relish his latest question.

"There are two ways I learned to bend time with Stranger," started Joan. "When I brought you and Aileen here, you experienced stepping from a moment to the same moment in another place. As I mentioned before, this is called warping.

"The second way I learned to bend time is as a means for concealment, sort of like a cloak. Though, it's not like the magic cloak of Harry Potter, or Frodo's enchanted ring, both of which render them invisible for sneaking around. Instead, I link with the moments in time around me, keeping the moments physically in front of me, behind me; the moments behind me, in front of me; to my left, on my right; and on my right, to my left. It's like taking the moments immediately surrounding my body and convincing them to swap places with each other. It creates the allusion that I'm not there at all, since anyone looking will see the moment, and view, immediately on the other side of me. This form of bending time is called obscuring. Watch and I'll show you."

Ko watched as Joan stood from her seat on the boulder. She took a step closer to the edge and remained facing him. He watched as a deep breath seemed to relax first her eyes, then her body. What happened next is what she had described. As she began pairing each moment in time around her with the inverse moment on each side of her body, she slowly began to disappear from his view, until at last there was a web rendering her entirely invisible from him. His mouth gaped as he watched.

"Well, what do you think?" said Joan.

Ko stood, sizing up the space where Joan had previously been, now an empty set of boulders where her voice was coming from. He took a step closer.

"Amazing. If I can't see you, how can I still hear you?"

"I'm still standing here. Obscuring doesn't stop sound, just changes what the eyes see. Bending time to obscure is more difficult than bending time to warp. It takes a more extended focus to maintain the obscure, whereas warping requires a sudden burst and then it's done," said Joan.

She dropped her obscure, revealing herself to Ko, who was once again amazed and overwhelmed by what he had witnessed.

"It's all so much. Everything you've told me, what you're showing me. My mind isn't sure where to go with all of it," said Ko.

"I know," said Joan.

Ko turned and looked toward Aileen again. He tried to orient himself to everything Joan had told him, everything he had witnessed, so he could decide what to do next. The only clear thought he could arrive at was that keeping Aileen safe was all that mattered. Past that, he wasn't sure of anything. He figured they could help Joan find the Quantum, and maybe by then he'd have some ideas on what to do next, and how to keep Aileen safe.

"So, what now?" said Ko. "You said this Quantum thing could help save your brother. Should we go back to Stono, or maybe our home in Chatuge to look for it? Does Stranger's book say what the device looks like?"

He began flipping through the pages of Stranger's book, scanning for clues. From her overalls, Joan pulled out the diamond necklace Ko's mother had left behind.

"Ko," said Joan.

He paused his flipping of the pages.

"I think this is the Quantum," said Joan.

She let the necklace fall and dangle from her fingers. The faded blue chains intertwined and twisted as the diamond spun back and forth.

"Your mother left it for me in Stono. I'm not sure how, but she knew I was in the room with her, your father, and the Scant. She made it clear that I was to take it after the Scant ... you know."

Ko was grateful at her tact in avoiding the details of how his parents had met the Veil.

"So, my mother's necklace is the Quantum. I wonder how it works. More than that, I wonder where Portum Lux is," said Ko, feeling uneasy.

He was wary of anything supernatural that might come with using a stone called a Quantum Device as a means for traveling to a place called Portum Lux.

"I don't know where, or what, Portum Lux is. All I know is without going there, I have no hope of saving Leo," said Joan.

"We're in," said Ko, catching Joan off guard.

"What do you mean, you're in?"

"Whatever the Quantum does, wherever Portum Lux is, we'll go there with you. If everything you've said is true, it'll be the safest thing for Aileen. We can't go back to our old life. I can't protect Aileen there."

"Huh, having company to Portum Lux hadn't really crossed my mind. Though, I suppose you may be right about it being the safest thing for Aileen." Joan pondered. "Okay then, you can come with me. Open the book back to the diagram referencing Portum Lux. The next page after that includes some sort of guide, or riddle, on how to use the necklace."

"You mean, how to use the Quantum?" said Ko with a smirk.

"Yes, the Quantum," Joan said with a small smile.

Ko stepped toward her while he opened the book to the marked page. He held the book so they could both examine the group of starry images once more. They followed the arrow from the stars to the words "Portum Lux," where another arrow picked up and guided them from the words "Portum Lux" to the edge of the page.

Ko turned the page, revealing more of Stranger's handwriting.

Wade in the shallow, clear above and clear below. Show me starlight, with one head breathing and one head drowning, and you will see a tunnel show. Enter the tunnel and to the haven you will flow, where Light is the only and Dark they do not know.

They sat silently for a minute, giving thought to what it meant, moving their eyes back and forth from the riddle to the necklace wrapped around Joan's hand.

"Does it make sense to you?" asked Ko.

"No, not really," said Joan.

"'Wade into the shallow.' So, we need to be in water," said Ko.

"'Clear above and clear below. Show me starlight.' It needs to be night and a clear sky," Joan mused thoughtfully.

"'One head breathing and one head drowning, and you will see a tunnel show.' What do you think that part means?" said Ko.

She shrugged her shoulders. They sat and pondered this part of the riddle in silence. Time passed as they sat on the boulder, each straining to think as clouds slowly rolled by overhead. Joan finally spoke.

"I think I know what it's asking us to do, but it's risky. Maybe the risk, in tandem with the diamond, is what brings the tunnel to us. If I'm right, then we need to find water, we need it to be night, and if we do it just right, a tunnel is going to appear that will take us to Portum Lux."

"Okay," Ko agreed. "It's getting dark now, so if we can find water, we can give it a shot. Do you know of any nearby?"

"Yeah, there's a river a few miles that way." She pointed across the field to where the clearing met a wall of trees breaking the continuity of mountains. "I can warp us there, or we can walk."

"Let's walk," Ko said quickly.

They left the boulders and walked back to Aileen. Joan stood back as Ko approached his sister, bending down and whispering in her ear.

"Aileen, how do you feel?"

"I feel fine, but I'm scared for Mom and Dad. I think something bad has happened." Aileen rolled over, her face a little pink and puffy from crying.

Hearing Aileen's words, and seeing where tears had streaked her cheeks, brought forth a well behind Ko's eyes. With a steady breath he maintained his composure, though seeing his sister's pain gripped and wringed his heart. He grabbed her hand, and with his other he brushed loose strands of hair from her face.

"I'm scared too, and I'm so sorry Mom and Dad aren't with us. Just know that I love you."

"I love you too."

"There's a lot that we need to talk about, but we don't have time right now. I need to introduce you to someone who we're going to go on a little adventure with. Is that okay?"

Aileen nodded and gracefully pulled herself out of the tall grass and back on her feet. Her golden hair streamed down blending in with the landscape. Holding hands, brother and sister walked toward Joan.

"Aileen, this is Joan. She saved us in Stono," said Ko.

Aileen stood close to Ko. Joan bent down a little so that she and the young girl were eye-to-eye.

"Aileen, it's very good to meet you. You're very pretty and very brave. I'd like to take you and your brother on an adventure to a safe place. How does that sound? Would you want to do that?"

Aileen sheepishly stared back at her.

"Are we going to look for Leo?" Aileen asked.

Joan was taken aback. She took a quick breath as if to respond but hesitated with her lips parted. She glanced at Ko, searching his face for a sign as to whether he had told Aileen about Leo. Ko could only offer a quick shrug and shake of the head. He was as surprised as Joan that Aileen knew about Leo.

Turning her attention back to Aileen and forcing a smile, Joan said, "Yes, we're going to look for Leo."

"Aileen, do you know Leo?" asked Ko.

"In a way," said Aileen.

"How?" said Ko.

"Like you said, we don't have time right now. We need to go," Aileen said decisively.

"She's right," chimed Joan. "We have endless unknowns that I'd be very grateful to spend time figuring out, but my only thought right now is finding Portum Lux and someone who can help us find Leo. I don't know what's become of him, and until I find out, the remaining questions we have for each other will have to wait."

Ko nodded in agreement. He realized now how patient Joan had been with him since Stono, explaining their circumstance and telling her story, all so he'd be up to speed enough to not hinder Joan's quest to save her brother. She must have been burning with urgency during the past hour or so, fighting the instinct to shake him and scream, "We need to go! We need to find Leo!"

Ko quieted his thoughts as they left the meadow. They walked silently as Joan led them to the woods. Joan indicated she had been there before and knew the woods would lead to a river. The sun had set, and their surroundings under the tree canopy had become dark.

They felt they weren't alone as the light faded. Trees swaying and branches creaking caused their eyes to dart left and right. Small animals running nearby sounded like footsteps. Each time the sound of footsteps fell, Ko and Joan would glance at each other. They walked through the woods toward the river as a child walks toward a bed at night: slowly at first, then quicker, and at last running until leaping into the bed to ensure nothing from beneath can grab legs.

Joan, Ko, and Aileen picked up the pace as the woods turned pitch black and the sound of footsteps grew louder. Finally, they broke into a sprint as the sound of water came near.

At last, they reached a clearing and the river. The sound of the river drowned out the imaginary footsteps that had chased them.

It was dark now, the clear sky of the mountains ushering in a host of stars. They approached the water and stood looking at it for a few minutes. Joan pulled Stranger's book out and recited the riddle, the quantum necklace dangling from her hand, as the three of them looked on.

"Wade in the shallow, clear above and clear below. Show me starlight, with one head breathing and one head drowning, and you will see a tunnel show. Enter the tunnel and to the haven you will flow, where Light is the only and Dark they do not know."

Ko knew what he had to do. He walked Aileen a few steps away and sat her down on a log, out of hearing range from the water's edge.

"I need you to stay here," said Ko.

Aileen nodded that she understood.

Returning to the water's edge, Ko drew close to Joan.

"I'll do it," said Ko.

"No," said Joan immediately, knowing what he meant. "I can't ask you to do that."

"It needs to be me." He swallowed hard. "If something goes wrong, you can do more for Aileen than I can. She'd be safer with you than me. Plus, it doesn't say I have to die; it just says one of us can't be breathing. If we push it, we can do this, and I'll be okay. You just have to be ready to pull me up," said Ko.

Joan knew Ko was right.

"Okay," she said.

They waded into the river, stopping waist deep in a pool where the water moved slowly. The river was fed by glacier water and was near freezing, with the bed of the pool visible at night with the starry sky. Aileen started to follow them, walking closer to the water and then stopping at the shore.

"Ko! What are you doing?" called Aileen across the water.

"It's okay. Stay there, don't move, and do whatever Joan tells you to. Do you understand?"

"Um, okay," Aileen said in an uneasy tone.

Ko hesitated before turning his attention back to Joan. He bent down, reaching under the water, feeling the bed of the river. After a few seconds of searching, he stood back up, straining to hold a large rock.

"Joan, between this rock and your foot, I need you to keep me under water until the tunnel shows. Don't let me up until then. Once the tunnel shows, you can pull me up," said Ko.

Joan nodded her head in agreement. Pulling the necklace out of her shirt, she let it fall down the front of her overalls, visible to the night sky. Joan looked from the diamond in the necklace back to Ko.

"Are you ready?" asked Joan.

Ko nodded yes. He leaned back and held the rock to his chest, letting his fall push him under the water. As he reached the bottom, Joan set her foot on the rock, applying enough pressure to keep him down. She could barely make out the shape of his face at the bottom of the pool. Tiny air bubbles began to trickle up to the surface.

Joan glanced from the necklace to the sky, then to the air bubbles. Nothing. Again, she looked from the necklace to the sky, then back to the air bubbles. The air bubbles were increasing. Again, she looked from the necklace to the sky, then back to the air bubbles. The air bubbles became a jet stream from the floor of the pool. Joan glanced at the necklace, but there was still nothing.

The air bubbles stopped. Joan felt Ko's weight shift and jerk under her foot. It was at this point that she heard something. She turned her attention to the sky. The sound was a buzz she couldn't comprehend through the noise of her adrenaline.

Finally, she realized the sound was Aileen screaming and sobbing from the river's edge.

"Ko! Pull him up!" repeated Aileen.

Joan felt the jerk of Ko's body subside. With no tunnel or Portum Lux in sight, she suddenly felt that it was wrong, that they had made a terrible mistake.

CHAPTER FIVE
PORTUM LUX

K o peacefully lay across the stone carpet of the river bottom. He was separated from the night sky by a few feet of water.

For a time, the air in his lungs supported his life. Inevitably this passed, and his body consumed the last of the air. Ko experienced the comfort of breathing give way to a drowning sensation. Though his body screamed for him to inhale, his awareness did not allow him to. The desire to breathe was outweighed by his mind's knowledge that a breath would be rewarded with water and not the air it desperately needed. Ko resisted his body's urge to breathe for as long as he could, while his blood flooded with carbon dioxide.

Not breathing meant certain death. Breathing in water meant certain death, but the sensation of not breathing at all was overwhelming. He broke. An involuntary breath brought a wave of water into his lungs. Another involuntary breath filled his lungs like a wineskin. He began to pass out as a burning sensation consumed his heart. The burning spread like a wildfire through his entire body. He tried to move the rock from his chest, but his body did not respond. He tried to shift his weight, but his muscles were constricted by what was now an all-consuming fire from his toes to his ears. His best effort was feeble. The night sky got darker. The burning sensation subsided, his eyes lost their sight, and the world faded to black.

There was no consciousness left to assess what came next. Thought and the sensation of being alive were reduced to something simpler: simply being gone.

Being gone faded to being black. Being black then faded to light. Ko didn't see light, nor feel the warmth of light, as he had lost the traditional senses associated with being alive. He couldn't see or feel. Instead of seeing or feeling light, Ko experienced becoming light, a transformation with no point of reference, as time no longer existed. Becoming light was like becoming the truth that connects the heart to the mind. In life, this truth sits on the top of the heart. It is rare, but a few times during life, the mind can look down and recognize the truth sitting on its heart. The transformation of becoming light is when, instead of looking at this truth, one's being enters inside the truth and remains.

As Ko's being moved from life to gone, gone to black, and black to light, the truth connecting his mind and heart remained. The truth inhaled what was formally his being and produced a peace. The peace began to produce a joy his former being had never known.

Joy was near Ko. It surrounded him. Then it stopped. It began to retreat. Peace and understanding retreated as well. His being couldn't comprehend what came next.

It was either the return of time or the return of being a being. Being a being again gave way to a burning sensation. The burning sensation gave way to an explosion of awareness, which seemed to start in the middle of consciousness and proliferate outward like an atom bomb. Thought and sight came last, followed by a violent episode of vomiting and coughing.

Ko lay on the bank of the river. Lying on his side, he continued to cough and convulse as Joan and Aileen kneeled next to him. They held and braced him any way they could. Each cough and expulsion of water from his lungs made way for what tasted like the sweetest air he had ever breathed. A few minutes passed, and the coughing subsided. Ko turned from his side to his back, once again looking at the night sky.

With Joan and Aileen's assistance, he was able to sit upright and lock his arms around his knees to keep from falling backward. Aileen and Joan stood, taking a step back to give him room.

Ko took a few more breaths and, clearing his throat, found his voice. He looked up at his sister and Joan.

"Well, did it work?" said Ko, his voice raspy.

Joan looked at him and then at the ground, shaking her head no.

"So, no tunnel? No Portum Lux?"

"No," said Joan.

Like Joan, Ko looked to the ground. What a waste, he thought to himself. He had almost left Aileen alone, for nothing.

"Ko, why did you do that?" said Aileen.

He looked up at Aileen. Her face was red with tears.

"Aileen, I'm sorry. I know it was scary and seemed strange. We thought what we were doing would cause the necklace to help us travel somewhere. Somewhere you'd be safe, and a place that would help Joan find her brother, Leo."

Aileen was unmoved by Ko's explanation.

"Did you do that because of what Joan's book said?"

"Yes," said Ko.

"You did it wrong," said Aileen.

"What? Did what wrong?" said Ko.

"The necklace. Joan's book says how to use it, but you didn't do it right," said Aileen.

Ko, still sitting, stared up at his younger sister. He turned to Joan with a look of wonder. Joan met the expression on his face with a similar one. They both looked back to Aileen, puzzled at what the young Celestial was saying.

Aileen turned to Joan and reached out her hand. "Can I see it?"

Joan handed the Quantum to Aileen. Ko stood as Aileen turned toward the water. Aileen pinned the diamond of the necklace between two fingers and held it close to her nose, turning it to examine each face of the gem. After a careful inspection, Aileen looked back at Ko and Joan, a sly smile creeping across her face.

"Are you ready?" said Aileen.

Joan and Ko, confused, nodded yes.

Aileen put the necklace around her neck, the blueish copper chain draping her small shoulders and the diamond falling to her belly. Wading into the water, Aileen began to recite the riddle from Stranger's book.

"Wade into the shallow, clear above and clear below," said Aileen.

The water rose above her waist. The night sky was clear above, and the water was clear below. Aileen took the diamond in her hand, holding it close to her face again, examining and turning the stone in her hands.

Stopping the rotation of the diamond, Aileen held it pinched between her fingers and recited the next part of the riddle. "Show me starlight, with one head breathing and one head drowning, and you will see a tunnel show."

Aileen held the diamond up to the sky, then lowered it into the water. She bent down, carefully holding the jewel, so only half of it was submerged. Aileen looked up and waited. Ko and Joan followed Aileen's gaze skyward. Nothing happened. But then, something did.

From a small black void in the sky, a light appeared. Faint at first, the light grew exponentially. In an instant, the light went from being distant to arriving at Aileen, presenting itself as a small beam.

The beam of light was so tiny it matched the diameter of the Quantum diamond. Appearing sturdy and full of power, the light paused just above Aileen, before completing its descent and settling on the Quantum diamond gently and silently. The light of the beam entered the top half of the diamond and refracted through the bottom half, which was still submerged by Aileen in the water. The light refracted through the lower half of the diamond, projecting a wider and circular pattern of light on the river's bottom. Aileen's feet fell within the circle of light, which began to get brighter.

Aileen finished the riddle. "Enter the tunnel and to the haven you will flow, where Light is the only and Dark they do not know."

Aileen took her eyes from the Quantum diamond and looked toward Ko and Joan, who remained motionless on the bank of the river.

"Follow me," said Aileen.

As soon as the words left Aileen's lips, a tunnel of light sprang from the floor of the pool, consuming Aileen. The tunnel shot into the night sky, consuming the path of the smaller beam that had preceded it. Ko and Joan watched as Aileen's figure became a shadow within the light, her body shimmering until it disappeared completely.

The tunnel of light remained. The space within the tunnel didn't appear to move at all. Ko couldn't tell if the tunnel led up into the sky or down deep into the earth.

Joan took a step into the water. Ko followed. They waded into the pool and approached the tunnel of light. Ko watched Joan as she sized the tunnel up. Joan's proximity to the light caused her eyes to flicker. Then, Joan stepped into the tunnel. Like Aileen, Joan's figure shimmered into a shadow and disappeared.

Ko took a final look around the dark wilderness surrounding him. In awe, he contemplated his circumstance. He felt a powerful urge to step into the tunnel of light and embrace their adventure, while a hint of nostalgia for his past and the world as he knew it caused him to hesitate slightly. The draw of the unknown and his love for Aileen won out, though it was never in doubt. Ko gave a nod to the wilderness, and like Joan and Aileen before him, he stepped into the tunnel of light.

They were no longer standing in water, and earth was no longer under their feet. There was nothing below them and nothing above, just outer space. The cylindrical wall of light encompassing their bodies acted as a lens to space. Moving too fast to make out solar systems or stars, only galaxies could be discerned before they, too, were left behind.

Focusing on the tunnel itself revealed the wall of light consisted of short glowing strands. The strands themselves were too small to see, but the glow from them revealed their varying lengths. Like the passing galaxies, each strand was left behind by their pace. The trio didn't realize it, but the glowing strands they were passing were the particles of light that made up the structure of the tunnel. Both the galaxies and the particles of light were beautiful to behold as they traveled past them.

Time passed as they crossed the universe, though moving at a quantum speed rendered the three travelers unable to sense it. Except for sight, and the sound of a dull white noise, the quantum travelers were devoid of sensation.

Suddenly, the tunnel went black. They felt solid ground under their feet once again. The tunnel of light was gone, leaving behind the glow of a circle imprinted on the ground where the three of them stood.

They didn't stop to think about how or why they had finished the trip standing upright. Had they given it thought, they would have realized the quantum tunnel of light had entered one side of the planet, passed them through head-first, and dumped them standing upright on the other side of the planet, where they now found themselves.

Ko, Aileen, and Joan took a few steps away from the tunnel's glowing imprint on the ground. They watched as the glow faded away, leaving behind a bare rock surface. The three of them looked at each other. Ko's jaw was open, Joan had a smirk, and Aileen was beaming a smile, looking back and forth between Ko and Joan.

"Did we all see the same thing? Was that real, the galaxies and everything?" said Ko.

"I think so," said Joan.

"That was amazing!" chimed Aileen.

They inventoried their surroundings. They were in the middle of an ocean. The ground they stood on was the rock of a tiny island. As far as they could see was water and sky. The planet looked and felt like Earth.

They walked the shoreline of the island. Straining their eyes across the ocean, they could see no other land. As they circled the island, they came upon a long wooden dock stretching out across the water. It was empty with no vessels tied to it. Continuing around the tiny island, they came across a second dock, then a third, and finally a fourth, each the same length. After passing the fourth dock, they arrived back where they had started. It hadn't taken them long to circle the entire island.

Turning to the center of the island, their eyes ventured upward. A tower of rock sheered vertically, its footprint taking up most of the island, and its base starting not far from the shoreline. Its circular shape was inconsistent, as certain sections had eroded away or collapsed. At the top they could barely make out what looked to be a structure. They continued around the base, surveying the insurmountable tower of rock, looking for a way up. Eventually, a small crevice in the rock caught their attention. Looking closer, they found a set of stairs cut in the rock, which spiraled upward. The three of them started up the stairs.

The steps were crude and uneven as they wrapped clockwise up the face of the rock tower. Ko led, with Aileen and Joan in tow. The brownish gray rock was on their right, and the expanse of an ocean was on their left. The higher they climbed, the slower they moved, careful to stay as close to the rock face as possible. In many locations, the stairs narrowed, bringing the ledge, and frightening falls, closer. They became concerned with how long it was taking them to reach the peak. The top had not seemed far from the ground, but the stairs had taken them around the entire perimeter of the island twice now, and there still seemed to be a substantial rise of rock above them. The structure was no longer visible as they looked up.

Finally, as they neared wrapping the island for a third time, the tower of rock gave way to a bald. The stairs straightened out toward the center of the bald, and the structure they had seen from the bottom came into full view. It was a lighthouse. An imposing structure, the lighthouse itself was very tall.

The stairs widened as they approached the base of the lighthouse. Stacked with white alabaster stone, the lighthouse had a circular footprint and produced the slightest of conical shapes as it rose from its rocky foundation. The stacked stone continued upward until giving way to a large wooden platform at its peak. The platform was enclosed with a railing and topped by a glass enclosure.

At the base of the lighthouse, where the top of the stairs finished, was a very tall entrance embedded in the white stone. The shape of the entrance was rectangular and capped with a high arch. Set back in the entry was a large white door, matching the height and shape of the arch. They reached the door. It was three times Ko's height. The three of them looked at each other and then back to the door.

"What do you think? Should we knock?" said Ko.

Aileen shrugged.

Joan, without saying anything, stepped in front of Ko and proceeded to hammer on the door with her right hand clenched in a fist.

They waited. After a few seconds, they could hear movement on the other side of the door. The sound got louder as it approached the door, then it stopped. Ko, Aileen, and Joan took a step back. What followed was a clinking and clanking coming from near the handle of the door. A clink would give way to a clank, then another clink, followed by a pause and then what sounded like muffled cursing through the door. Each time there was a clink or a clank, the muffled cursing grew louder. Finally, the clinking and clanking gave way to a loud TINK. The cursing stopped and then there was a creaking sound as the door slowly swung open.

The open door of the lighthouse revealed a man standing in front of the three travelers. He was an older gentleman and stood at an average height. His head was topped with white frazzled hair. His forehead was wrinkled, sun worn, and topped a pair of wild eyebrows that acted like awnings for two beady eyes buried between his forehead and cheeks. The man's nose was nondescript but was a tad long from age. The space between his nose and mouth was filled with a large bushy mustache, which covered the corners of his lips and branched down his cheeks, finishing at his chin. The mustache was darker than the white hair on his head. His jaw was square. He wore a white linen suit joined to his neck by a dark bow tie. The linen suit fit loosely, with the pants finishing just above a pair of brown leather shoes. His beady eyes gave off the slightest twinkle before going dark once again.

CHAPTER SIX
TOURLITIS

"Well, state your business," he barked.

Ko, Aileen, and Joan glanced at each other, caught off guard and unsure of how to respond. Their hesitation caused the man to impatiently wriggle his jaw, ruffling his mustache.

"If I had all the time in the universe, I'd love to stand here all day and wait for you to find your tongues, but as it is, I don't have all the time in the universe. So, pipe up or pipe off!" said the man.

"Is this Portum Lux?" said Joan.

"What kind of question is that, little girl? Of course this is Portum Lux," said the man.

Joan let out a short sigh of relief before continuing, "We need help."

"Mmmph, need help. Every being in the universe needs help. Why should I help you?" said the man.

Aileen stepped forward and pulled the quantum necklace from around her neck. She held it out to the man in the doorway.

"All we have is our need. That should be enough for you to help us," said Aileen.

The man's face softened as he took the quantum necklace from Aileen and examined the diamond. "Where did you get this?" he asked.

"We'll tell you if you let us in," said Joan.

The man glanced between Joan and Aileen before nodding and stepping to the side, allowing space for Ko, Aileen, and Joan to enter the lighthouse.

Once inside, they found themselves in a large open room with a great space above, which extended to the bottom of the lighthouse pinnacle. The lighthouse had looked tall from the outside, but it looked even taller from the inside. The perimeter consisted of small rooms with vertical stone walls terminating into the structure's conical shell, the entry to each room guarded by a dark wooden door.

They followed the man in white to the far end of the hall where seating was staged around a large unlit fireplace. The floor consisted of a jigsaw patterned granite floor joined together by grout. Though the air was warm, the stone floor felt cold. The man took a seat in a wooden rocking chair near the fireplace and motioned for the three of them to follow suit. They did as they were asked and settled in, positioning themselves on a long leather couch across from the linen-clad man, now rocking slowly across from them.

"Well?" said the man as he continued to examine the quantum diamond in his hands, turning it between his fingers.

"Joan?" said Ko, signaling for Joan to take the lead.

Joan looked back at Ko and nodded her head in agreement. Joan proceeded to tell the man everything that had happened.

She told the man about her parents, about Leo, about Stranger, the Scant taking Leo, how Joan used Stranger's book to seek out the quantum necklace. She recounted how, after finding Ko and Aileen's parents, the Scant showed up again, prompting her to save Ko and Aileen from the Scant. Joan relayed that she herself was an Arc. She suspected Ko was an Arc too, and believed Aileen to be a Celestial like her brother. Finally, she revealed how they used Stranger's book and the quantum diamond to travel to Portum Lux in hopes of saving Leo.

The man in linen continued rocking in his chair as he listened to Joan recount the events. He remained quiet and looked past her as she spoke, his face unmoved. When Joan finished telling their story, the man stopped rocking. His face, previously stoic, now gave way to concern as he leaned forward. Ko, Aileen, and Joan leaned forward as well in anticipation of how the man would respond to their story.

He stroked his mustache and said, "I must say, I have not heard such a grave and daring tale in quite some time. I'm Sam, the Steward of Portum Lux, and I will help you."

The three of them looked at each other in relief.

"There are some things you need to understand about who you are and what it is that's happening to you. First, I imagine you're hungry. I'll be right back," said Sam.

Sam stood and walked across the hall of the lighthouse, disappearing into one of the rooms along the perimeter. After a minute or two, he emerged from the room with a tray in hand. Walking back to where they were sitting, he set the tray on a table in front of them. The tray was lined with cheese, sliced meats, and steaming hot bread. Picking up a pitcher from the tray, he poured each of them a glass of water before setting the pitcher back down and returning to his rocking chair.

"Please. Help yourselves," said Sam.

Before now, they hadn't realized how hungry they were or how long it had been since they had eaten. They set upon the food with urgency.

"While you stuff your faces, I need you to pay attention to what I'm about to tell you. If there's any chance for you, Joan, to save Leo, then you need to listen carefully. Understand?" said Sam.

Sam had assumed a serious tone to accompany the concern that had crept across his face. The three of them nodded their heads yes, their mouths too full to speak.

"Good," said Sam.

Sam leaned back in his rocking chair, allowing his weight to set it in motion once again. What came next from Sam was the true story of creation, the universe, and the battle between Light and Dark.

"Before creation, before the beginning, a singular being of Light presided. In a way, before the beginning of the universe, there was no beginning, just Light. The way of Light was even and balanced across all the would-be dimensions. More than a physical balance of light and warmth, the being of Light projected a feeling of peace, the kind our hearts and minds are capable of only catching a glimpse of.

"Imagine a perfect tone of white light, the warmth of a spring day with a light breeze, and your heart and mind being in perpetual comfort and joy. That was the being of Light before creation.

"The being of Light knew and constantly experienced perfection. However, the perfection was singular. Light began to seek a new kind of perfection, one that could be experienced separate and outside of itself. In a way, Light sought to share its perfection with something, or someone. To do so, Light divided itself, allowing the first of all created beings.

"Light named the being Dark.

"The creation of Dark sparked the beginning of the universe, space, and time. Of course, there was a period where Light and Dark were alone with each other. They were happy together, harmonious in space and time. Dark sought to fill space, creating voids where it pleased Light. The voids created by Dark allowed Light to pursue its new perfection.

"You see, the being of Light was so pure and intense that nothing could exist next to it except Dark. The creation of Dark allowed a buffer between Light and other things. With Dark in place and distances established, Light initiated life in the universe. Life, as designed by Light, produced a new wave of beings with which Light could be in relationship with.

"The protection of this life was championed by Dark and its darkness. If the being of Light, in its purest form, came into contact with life, the fabric of life would disintegrate and dissolve into nothing. If not for Dark's presence, life as we know it would not have been possible.

"Time passed, and the life Light had sowed began to flourish. Through the partnership of Light and Dark, embryonic life began to populate the universe. Embryonic life, as evidenced by the world in which the three of you are from,"—Sam raised his hand in a gesture toward them—"produced great beauty. Beings continued to evolve, reflecting the image of Light more and more, and making the joy of Light more and more complete.

"However, as time went on, Dark observed the relationship between Light and life, and jealousy was born. Seeing the pleasure

Light found in life made Dark long to be the pleasure of Light instead. This longing drove Dark to seek elimination of life in order to return existence back to when Dark was first created, when there was only Light and only Dark, alone together.

"Light perceived Dark's desire and rebuked Dark. Light's rebuke of Dark created a chasm between the two, with Dark being condemned to dwell in the bowels of the universe.

"However, the story of Dark did not end with its banishment by Light. Dark fought back, sending the universe and all of creation into chaos. This state of chaos, and the push and pull between Light and Dark, is what the three of you find yourselves in. Any questions so far?"

Wide eyed and still stuffing their faces, the three of them slowly shook their heads no. Sam twitched his mouth back and forth, to ruffle his unkempt mustache into an acceptable state, before continuing on.

"After Dark's banishment, Light set life on a new course. One where life could evolve to a state of independence from Dark, allowing life to dwell in direct contact with Light.

"This evolution of life, one where beings crescendo to a state of existence that no longer requires the buffer of darkness, will be complete when Light undoes the voids of the universe, eliminating the being of Dark and allowing the beings of life to dwell in a new perfection with Light. Of course, Light is the only one who knows when the evolution of life will be complete. Until then the universe is expanding, and life is flourishing under the stewardship of Light.

"The expanding universe contains many beings that have spawned from life. The most evolved of these beings are Celestials. Celestials are the greatest joy of Light and capable of communicating with and traveling with Light. Beyond their connection with Light, Celestials are also the most essential to life reaching Light's ultimate goal. To capture the importance of Celestials to Light, it's necessary now to discuss what happened to the jealous being of Dark after it was rebuked by Light.

"Banished and in the depths of the universe, Dark simmered with anger as it observed Light and Celestials flourishing. Dark thought of removing its darkness from the universe, the protection that allowed life to exist, but could not without Light returning to its original state and in turn Dark ceasing to exist. With no other options, Dark suffered and watched from afar, waiting for its inevitable demise. However, after eons of distant observation, Dark noticed something peculiar regarding the relationship between Light and Celestials.

"When Light divided itself and created the universe, it divided its very being across the universe. Each galaxy, and its glow, represents a small piece of the being of Light. As part of Light's plan, its most evolved beings, Celestials, are each connected with a galaxy.

"That is to say, the peculiar something Dark learned after eons of observation was that each Celestial is a galaxy somewhere in the universe, and a conduit to the being of Light. In ways we can't understand, the dependence between a Celestial and its galaxy is part of Light's design for life, and key to life's evolution towards Light's ultimate purpose."

Joan interrupted, "Sam, you're saying that each Celestial belongs to a galaxy. Or, are you saying each galaxy in the universe belongs to a Celestial?"

"It is both, as a Celestial and its galaxy are one in the same," responded Sam. "Let me fetch something I think will help illustrate this for you."

Sam stood from his chair and shuffled to another room. He opened the door and vanished among what looked to be stacks of books.

Joan turned to Ko and Aileen. "That's it. What Stranger kept from Leo and me, the secret regarding Celestials and Light. Aileen, like Leo, you are the heart of a Galaxy somewhere in the universe."

Before Aileen or Ko could respond, Sam came shuffling back, holding a large and dusty black leather book. He handed it to Joan, who needed Ko's help to lift it. Joan and Ko brushed the dust from the book, as Aileen tried to blow the dust away before it could settle on her. Sam settled back in his chair.

"What you now hold is a record of known Celestial-galaxy pairings. It contains fairly accurate illustrations and depictions of each pair, as well as important information about the Celestials themselves and the location of their galaxies."

Joan began to flip through the book, taking care to turn each large page without a tear. In addition to short biographical accounts, and long strings of numbers and symbols which looked to be coordinates, each page revealed black and white illustrations of a Celestial, as well as a depiction of the Celestial's galaxy. The Celestial portraits showed men and women from different ages, each with a look that seemed to match their time. The galaxies were rendered as if being viewed from afar. Spirals and discs were the most common shapes, though some of the galaxies were illustrated as irregular and non-symmetrical.

"Does this contain all Celestials?" asked Joan, looking up from the pages and back to Sam.

"No, that volume is one of thousands," said Sam.

"It's amazing, to learn the truth about Celestials and galaxies. Knowing it changes everything," said Joan.

"Amazing indeed," Sam echoed wistfully, "and for a long time it was a great secret. Which brings us back to Dark, who discovered this great secret in the cruelest of ways.

"Dark theorized and hatched an experiment. The experiment took place long ago, and it involved the capture of a Celestial by Dark. Dark imprisoned the Celestial in a part of the universe known as the Aphotic. The Aphotic is a dimension of the universe where no light exists, and darkness is perpetual. It resulted from Light's original banishment of Dark, as the actual being of Dark could no longer be near Light and required somewhere else to go. The Aphotic is where the being of Dark went, leaving behind only its darkness in the universe.

"After imprisoning its first Celestial, Dark did nothing but sit back and watch what came next. The Aphotic, originally intended to allow a space where Dark could be completely separate from Light, started to have the same 'completely separate' effect on the relationship between the Celestial, its galaxy, and the being of Light.

"In time, the bond between the captured Celestial and its galaxy completely dissolved. As soon as the bond was gone, the Celestial and its galaxy were extinguished. In an instant, all the solar systems and stars belonging to that galaxy were put out, and their light was no more. The result was catastrophic. The being of Light felt something it had never experienced: loss. Life in the universe and the fabric of space were suddenly in jeopardy. Worse than anything, the being of Dark was emboldened, as it had found a way to extinguish light. No longer did Dark have to wait for its inevitable demise. Through the imprisonment of Celestials in the Aphotic, Dark could slowly extinguish the galaxies of the universe, in turn slowly destroying the being of Light, until there was no light left, and Dark would preside over existence alone."

"Sam," Aileen politely cut into the account of Dark's great revelation.

Sam's work-like tone softened as he responded to Aileen, "Yes, dear?"

"Do you have any more of that hot bread? As you can see, we've eaten it all, and as I believe it to be the most delicious bread I've ever had, I sure would welcome some more, if it's not a bother."

Sam's gruff was no match for Aileen's sweetness. His eyes moved from Aileen to the now empty tray that sat before them, then back to Aileen.

"Of course," said Sam. He quickly retreated with the empty tray and then returned it full once again with hot bread, though it was absent of meat and cheese this time.

"Is this to your liking, my dear?" said Sam as he set the tray down before them.

"Very much so. Thank you," said Aileen as she happily picked up a piece and took a grand bite.

With the hint of a smile, Sam resumed his seat. Though the smile faded as he picked up where he had left off, detailing what had happened after Dark's victory in destroying its first Celestial.

"After the first Celestial was lost, a war ensued, which resulted in the advent of Arcs and Scants. The war that took place is known as the Nebula Encounters.

"You see, young Celestials are referred to as Nebulas. Older Celestials are known as Quasars. A Quasar, or a fully matured Celestial, is fully connected with Light and untouchable by Dark. Dark is unable to capture and take a Quasar to the Aphotic. However, a Nebula, or young Celestial, is still growing in its connection to the being of Light and vulnerable to the power of Dark. Hence, the war was named the Nebula Encounters, as Dark sought out Nebulas for capture and imprisonment in the Aphotic until the Nebulas and their young galaxies were extinguished.

"In response to Dark's actions, Light began pairing Celestials with siblings now known as Arcs. Light gave Arcs command over time as a weapon to be used in protecting Celestials from Dark.

"Dark recruited beings of its own, called Scants. Scants are wayward beings, originally created by Light, having wandered from good and fallen under the influence of Dark. Scants have access to the Aphotic and can travel between it and the rest of the universe. The more consumed by Dark a Scant becomes, the greater that Scant's link with the Aphotic becomes. It's a Scant's link to the Aphotic that provides the Scant with power. A Scant's power consists of the ability to travel the universe in an instant wherever there's darkness, and the power to hold a lesser being captive in its presence. All Scants carry a black Veil provided to them by Dark, which serves as their portal to the Aphotic and the source of their power."

"I felt that in Stono," interjected Ko, "with the Scant. I couldn't move when it looked at me. Why is that, Sam?"

Ko glanced between Joan and Sam as he spoke.

"A Scant's eyes can see fear. Not in the way that we see someone who looks scared. Scants actually see the fear, can behold it within someone. The fear responds to the Scant's gaze and holds its host hostage. It was your fear, Ko, which the Scant preyed on," said Sam.

A rush came over Joan as she realized this is what had happened to her when facing the Scant, as Leo was being consumed by the Veil.

"It makes sense. When Leo was taken, I couldn't move to save him. I thought it was me. I guess it was me, it was my fear the Scant used to paralyze me. How do you beat it, Sam?" said Joan.

"When facing a Scant, you must be empty of fear. It's safest for the heart to be empty of everything, even love, as love can breed anxiety and longing, which is a second cousin to fear and terror. It doesn't mean you can't face a Scant with love in your heart; it's just dangerous. Now, I must return to the story of Dark for your benefit. The power of a Scant's gaze over fear can wait until later, okay?"

Joan and Ko nodded their heads, and Sam resumed his account of Light and Dark.

"The Nebula Encounters waged on between Light and Dark, Arcs and Scants, over the prized beings of the universe, Celestials. If a Scant captured a Celestial before it became a Quasar, and imprisoned the young Celestial in the Aphotic, then a small piece of Light's being was lost forever. If a Nebula Celestial was protected long enough, until it became a Quasar, the Celestial grew so close to Light that it was forever safe from Dark and its Scants. Further, once becoming a Quasar, a Celestial can use light to combat Scants.

"The Nebula Encounters saw many Celestials and their galaxies lost to the Aphotic. The very existence of good and light came close to being no more as the Scants slowly extinguished quadrants of the universe. At last, a brave band of Arcs and Quasars mounted an offensive against the Scants of Dark. A great battle ensued and brutally finished with the defeat of the Scants. The majority of the Scants fell to the Arcs and Quasars, with only a handful retreating to the Aphotic and escaping destruction. The war was finished, and Dark was defeated.

"Since the war, Scant activity in the universe has been rare. This makes your story and the capture of your brother most concerning, as it has been some time since the capture of a Nebula has been reported."

Joan's body stiffened. "Wait, you said that young Celestials, I mean Nebulas or whatever, are extinguished in the Aphotic. Leo is a young Celestial. What does this mean for him? Is he a Nebula? He's been taken by that Scant. Is he in the Aphotic? We need to do something! We need to find my brother! You said you could help!"

"My girl, I'm sorry for what I'm about to say, but your brother has certainly been taken to the Aphotic, and I know of no way to save him from that place. It takes time for the Aphotic to break a Celestial, so your brother is not gone yet, but unfortunately, in the history of existence, a Celestial has never been rescued from the Aphotic. While your brother has time yet, he's out of reach of anything we can do for him. However, I said I would help you, and that I will. Just before you arrived there was another arrival on Portum Lux. If anyone can tell us how to save your brother from the Aphotic, before he and his galaxy are extinguished, it will be the being who arrived just before you did." said Sam.

"Where is this being now? Take me there!" said Joan. Tears filled the corners of her eyes as she stood.

"I'm going with you," said Ko, leaving his seat to stand beside Joan.

Aileen stood as well, as if to say she wouldn't be left behind.

"Slow down, my young travelers," said Sam as he eyed Ko and Aileen. "The two of you are not going where Joan is going. Joan was right earlier when she said that you, Ko, are an Arc, and that you, Aileen, are a Celestial. I can also sense that Joan is advanced for a young Arc and ready to travel with me. Ko, you, on the other hand, need training. Aileen, you are a Nebula and need nothing but time and to remain in Portum Lux where you are safe. One day you'll be a Quasar and able to travel the universe as you please, without fear of Scants."

Sam stood. He glanced around the lighthouse as he shook his linen suit, adjusting the fit.

"The isle we're on is called Tourlitis and is the entrance to Portum Lux. It is to the other isles of Portum Lux that we must go. In order to do so, we will need ships."

"Wait," said Joan.

"Yes?" said Sam.

"Are you an Arc?" said Joan.

"Yes," said Sam.

"Why do we need ships, then? I'm sure you've been to the places we need to go. Can you not warp us there? We don't have time to lose," said Joan.

"While I am an Arc, young girl, it has been so long since I've warped anywhere that I'm afraid I don't remember how. If I tried to warp you anywhere, we could end up suspended in space, or at the bottom of the ocean. The ships are safer, trust me," said Sam.

Joan didn't press further.

Seeing that Joan was content with his response, Sam walked to a spiral staircase adjacent to the large unlit fireplace and began ascending the stairs. Ko, Aileen, and Joan followed. The staircase led to the lantern room of the lighthouse. Once Sam reached the top, he unlatched an access door in the ceiling and pushed it open. Light poured in from the open hatch. They each stepped and pulled themselves up through the hatch and into the top of the lighthouse. Once they were all clear of the hatch, Sam closed it, completing the wooden floor on which they now stood.

The lantern room was circular, enclosed by windows, and capped by a high copper ceiling. In the center of the room, above eye level, sat the beacon of the lighthouse, though it was not lit. The beacon consisted of a spinning prism enclosed in a fixed glass sphere. A copper tube ascended above the beacon, connecting it to the pinnacle of the lighthouse.

The four of them slowly walked along the perimeter of the lighthouse, looking out across the empty ocean that sprawled before them. Sam turned his attention back to the center of the room. He located a ladder and positioned it under the beacon. Leaving the ladder, Sam walked across the room and located a long pole with a hook. He took a few steps up the ladder with the pole and, reaching the pole up past the beacon, located a knob on the copper tube that led from the beacon to the pinnacle of the lighthouse. Placing the hook carefully on the knob, Sam gave a quick pull, opening an internal shutter within the copper tube. Immediately, light flooded in from the sky of Portum Lux, and through the spinning prism. The result was a solid beam of light bleeding forth from the prism and across the landscape of Portum Lux in a circular pattern. Sam returned the ladder and pole to their places, then motioned for Aileen, Joan, and Ko to join him once again in a slow walk around the perimeter of the lighthouse.

Sam paused and looked down at one of the long wooden docks below. The three travelers followed suit. The four of them let their eyes follow the line of the dock out into the water, and beyond.

A faint flash of light greeted them on the horizon. After a few seconds, the flash of light returned, and again a few seconds later. It was another lighthouse responding to the signal from Tourlitis.

"Aileen, you'll be traveling to the Isle of Skye. The Isle of Skye belongs to the Celestials," said Sam.

They then moved ninety degrees, counterclockwise around the perimeter of the lighthouse, to the next dock. There they found another flash of light on the horizon.

"Ko, you'll be traveling to the Isle of Eclaireur. The citadel from the Nebula Encounters is there. It is where you'll be introduced to bending time as an Arc," said Sam.

Sam walked, and they followed, another ninety degrees around the perimeter of the lighthouse before stopping and looking down at a third dock. They observed a third periodic flash of light every few seconds from the horizon beyond the third dock.

"Joan, you and I will be visiting the Isle of Mouro together. The being I spoke of, who arrived today, is there. It's there, and with that being, we'll seek out the secrets of the Aphotic and learn whether or not your brother can be saved," said Sam.

Sam continued to walk along the exterior. Joan, Ko, and Aileen stayed back, mesmerized by the flashing light coming from the Isle of Mouro.

"What now?" Ko said softly, out of earshot from Sam.

"We do what Sam says," replied Joan. "Aileen will be safe on Skye, you'll train and become a true Arc on Eclaireur, and I'll find a way to save Leo on Mouro."

"If you discover a way to your brother, to the Aphotic or whatever, promise you'll come and find me on Eclaireur, and we'll go after him together. If my parents were taken where your brother is, I need to be there," said Ko.

"I'll discover a way, and I promise to find you when I do," said Joan, her voice full of resolve."

"What about me? Can I go?" said Aileen.

"If you left Portum Lux, then who would eat all of the hot bread?" Ko said with a smirk.

Aileen smiled. "That's a good point, but I'm worried about the two of you. What if you need me?"

Joan watched as Ko put an arm around his sister and pulled her close.

"Don't worry. I won't be gone long, and neither will Joan. We both plan to make quick work of Mouro and Eclaireur, after which we'll all be together again. Isn't that right, Joan?"

"That's right," said Joan as she gave Aileen a smile.

Aileen seemed content with their assurances and remained silent as she leaned under Ko's arm.

Joan and Ko exchanged an apprehensive but warm glance. They knew their futures were uncertain, and that there was no guarantee they'd all see each other again.

Turning their focus to the distant lighthouses, a few minutes passed before three small specks appeared on the horizon. A few more flashes from the distant lighthouses came and went before the specks arrived at Tourlitis. The specks were ships.

CHAPTER SEVEN
MOURO

Gashed sails and torn nets adorned the old wooden ship on which Joan and Sam now stood. There was no crew and no captain, just Joan and Sam. Still docked at the Isle of Tourlitis, Joan and Sam had just finished watching Ko's and Aileen's ships disappear into the horizon: Ko to the Isle of Eclaireur and Aileen to the Isle of Skye. Once Ko and Aileen were no longer in view, the ship destined for the Isle of Mouro gave a shudder and drifted away from its dock.

Based on the ship's appearance, Joan thought it entirely possible that a band of pirates would appear from the hull and take control of it, but no pirates showed. Instead, the empty ship began to move forward, leaving the dock and the Isle of Tourlitis behind. The ship sailed perfectly straight, unmoved by the rolling ocean. Its rigid posture was locked in by a tractor beam-like force, as if a magnet were pulling it toward its destination instead of wind.

Sam leaned with his back against the railing of the ship. He watched as Joan impatiently paced from one side of the quarter deck to the other.

Her mind was consumed with fear as she contemplated the Aphotic. Sam had described the Aphotic as a dimension of the universe where light didn't exist. She was scared for her brother and scared of the story Sam had told, a story where Nebulas like Leo were taken to the Aphotic and held captive until they were extinguished. Joan didn't have the capacity to care about the galaxy connected to Leo that was at risk of being destroyed. She just wanted Leo back by her side. She didn't care if light didn't exist in the Aphotic. Leo was in the Aphotic, and she was going to find him. Joan stopped her nervous pacing and instead walked across the ship's deck to Sam.

"How long does my brother have?" said Joan.

Sam's white hair and dark mustache blew wildly with the wind.

"I don't know, my girl. From your story, he's been in the Aphotic now for a few days. Some Nebulas last a week in the Aphotic, others a month, and still others have lasted a few months before being extinguished. It depends on the mettle of the Nebula," said Sam.

The tone of inevitability in Sam's response caused Joan's face to sink. Sam, perceiving the effect his statement had on Joan, worked to undo his words and raise Joan's hopes.

"Though, my girl, from what I can tell about you, I'd say your brother's mettle will be up to the test. If he's anything like you, he'll give the Aphotic and that Scant a run for their money like they've never seen before."

Sam's words drew a forced smile from Joan. But the smile faded quickly from her face. She stepped to the side and leaned against the railing alongside Sam, each of them looking across the quarter deck of the ship. Both the clear sky above and the tall waves below felt gentle, and they seemed to saunter by though the ship was moving fast. Sam could tell his words had done little to lift the despair Joan was feeling for her brother. He sought to lift her spirits.

"Joan the Arc. It has a nice ring to it, you know, though it sounds familiar, don't you think?" said Sam.

Sam knew Joan of Arc's story well but was coy in his comment. He hoped referencing the young French maiden would stoke Joan's mind and distract her from brooding.

"You're referring to Joan of Arc," said Joan. "My parents named me after her. The Arc piece is a coincidence."

"Yes, that's right, Joan of Arc," said Sam, as if he had just grasped the significance of Joan's namesake. "I'm familiar with Joan of Arc's story. The teenage girl who fearlessly and supernaturally led armies of men to victory. Your parents did well to name you after her. Did you know that Joan of Arc is the only military leader in history, of either sex, to hold supreme military command at the age of seventeen?"

This last comment gave away his intentions to distract her. She was disinterested in engaging further with him, preferring to quietly wait for the Isle of Mouro.

"Joan of Arc is a nice story but not real. Yes, a young girl lived and paraded around with the French army for a year or so, while they inevitably won some battles on their home turf, but I don't believe Joan of Arc was truly the supreme leader of the military, talking with God and having visions before each victory. If Joan of Arc was truly connected with God and beloved by her people, then she wouldn't have been captured, abandoned by the French, and burned at the stake. She was nothing more than a political and religious prop used by the French to scare the English and give hope to the less educated masses," said Joan, confident she had done enough to kill the topic with Sam.

Sam was unmoved by Joan. Her disinterest and dissent on the topic did not have its intended effect.

"Ah, so you think you know the story of Joan of Arc. It's quite apparent you don't know anything. You're correct in saying that Joan of Arc was a real girl, but after that you've gotten it all wrong about the greatest warrior to ever grace the universe. In fact, your history books have gotten most of it wrong when it comes to Joan of Arc. That's to be expected, however. Neither you nor your history books could have known any better, so you are not to blame. That said, I'll look past your ignorance and will now set upon fixing your distorted view towards the phenomenon that is Joan of Arc."

Sam paused to ruffle his windblown mustache.

"It's said that Joan of Arc's supernatural powers brought the French victory. The French called these supernatural powers God, while the English called Joan a sorceress. The French and the English did not agree on much, especially during those times, but one thing the French and English agreed on was that Joan of Arc was burned at the stake.

"This is not true. Joan of Arc was not burned at the stake. She only let it appear that she was burned at the stake to fool both the French and the English. The truth is that Joan of Arc used her sway over time to create the allusion that she died at the stake. You see, my girl, your namesake Joan of Arc was in fact an Arc, like you. How else do you think she defeated a world power like the English?"

"You're lying. It's clever, but please don't treat me like a child," snapped Joan.

Sam acted as if he hadn't heard her.

"The young French maiden had a little brother named Pierre who was a Celestial. The Hundred Years War wasn't about French independence but was instead one of many battles in The Nebula Encounters where a Celestial, in this case Pierre, was protected from the advances of Scants. Once Pierre was safe, Joan of Arc allowed that farce of a trial and her conviction by the English to take place as a cover for what had really taken place. Once tied to the stake, Joan of Arc created an obscure and then warped out of France, leaving the flame behind and the mob none the wiser. From that point forward, Joan of Arc, the young French maid believed to be dead, traveled the universe as one of the greatest Arc warriors in the Nebula Encounters. You say it's a coincidence you share the same name with Joan of Arc, but now you know that it's no coincidence. Joan of Arc was like you, Joan the Arc."

Joan struggled to respond. She wanted to rebuke Sam further for being a crazy old man, but part of her felt that Sam's outlandish story was true.

As Joan started to speak, she felt the ship drag as it slowed. Leaving her post on the railing, she walked to the bow and stood facing their destination. The Isle of Mouro was a large dark mound which seemed to expand before her eyes as the ship drew closer. On top of the mound rested a proportionately large dark structure. The sprawling edifice was built into the black earth of Mouro. At a distant corner of the isle, a light would periodically flash. The flash belonged to the lighthouse of Mouro, which corresponded with the lighthouse of Tourlitis.

Sam climbed the bow of the ship and stood next to Joan.

"Joan, it is here on the Isle of Mouro, the universe's prison for Scants, where the answer lies as to whether your brother Leo can be saved or not," said Sam.

Joan glanced at Sam, speechless, before turning her attention back to the dark prison, which with each second consumed more and more of Joan's view. As they drew close, Joan felt the effects of the Scant prison.

The isle had a strange mix of light and dark. It appeared as if shadows were continuously failing to light, but without the shadows ever fully disappearing. She could sense the torture its inhabitants were experiencing, so far removed from the darkness for which they longed. Anxiety struck Joan as she remembered being paralyzed by the Scant's gaze. She didn't want to admit it, but she was scared of so many things, and what she feared most was that she wouldn't be brave enough to face a Scant and save Leo.

"Sam, what if a Scant sees me? I think it will happen again."

"Don't worry, the Scants are severed from their powers on Mouro. Their gaze will have no effect on you," Sam said reassuringly.

Reaching the port, Joan and Sam descended from the ship onto a long wooden dock, like the one from which they had departed on Tourlitis. They walked along the dock until reaching the black rock, which made up the mass of Mouro. It was there where they were greeted by a radiant figure.

The radiant figure belonged to Andromeda, a Quasar Celestial presiding as steward of the Isle of Mouro. Andromeda was an older-looking man whose appearance still gave off youth and strength. With dark skin, dark eyes, a shaved head, and a tall but broad build, Andromeda had an imposing presence. He wore white garments that overlapped as a sort of robe.

"Andromeda," said Sam.

"Sam," said Andromeda. His voice was deep and stern, his face stoic.

Joan stood by as Sam and Andromeda proceeded to stare each other down in silence. Joan became nervous as time passed, because the greeting did not appear to be courteous.

At last, a smile broke on Sam's face, which was met with a smirk by Andromeda. The two hugged, with the large radiant figure engulfing the old linen-clad man. Joan felt relief.

"Old friend, it is good to see you," said Andromeda, his voice booming as he pulled away from Sam.

"You as well," Sam said gruffly.

Sam motioned for Joan to come closer. She obeyed and stepped toward Andromeda.

"Andromeda, meet Joan the Arc. Joan, meet Andromeda the Quasar and steward of Mouro," said Sam.

Joan reached out her small arm, which was swallowed by the large dark hands of Andromeda.

"It is a pleasure to meet you," said Andromeda.

The young tomboy Arc stared up at him.

"It's a pleasure to meet you as well," said Joan.

"I know why you are here," said Andromeda.

"You do?" Joan asked.

"Yes. You're here because your brother Leo has been taken to the Aphotic."

"That's right. I plan to save him." said Joan, forcing an assertion into her tone to show the Quasar she wasn't afraid.

"Child, your will is strong. I can tell you have the same fire that lies within your brother. I'm sorry for your loss. It has been centuries since a Nebula was taken to the Aphotic, and this sudden rise in Scant activity is a grave concern for the universe. Between the Scant who took your brother and the new arrival here on Mouro, there's reason to believe that Dark is gaining strength," said Andromeda.

Andromeda's attention moved from Joan to the sky as he spoke, as if he were looking for motion among the cosmos.

"How do you know my brother? Why do you say he is lost?" The rise in Joan's voice revealed a despair her composure failed to contain. Her small figure had stiffened toward Andromeda as she continued to stare up at him.

"I'm the same as your brother, a Celestial. I've always known him, and I feel him even as we speak. I say that your brother is lost because I don't believe he can be saved. No one, except for a Scant, can travel to the Aphotic, where your brother is now held prisoner," said Andromeda.

"You can feel Leo?" said Joan.

"I can feel his galaxy and the light within it. The light is fading, but slowly," said Andromeda.

"Can you feel how much time he has?" said Joan.

Joan was afraid of what the answer would be.

"He's resisting the Aphotic well. The light of his galaxy is still strong, but time can be a strange thing in the universe. Speaking in terms of time from your world, Leo has two orbits of your moon before he and his galaxy will be destroyed by the Aphotic," said Andromeda.

"So, two months, right?" said Joan.

Joan looked at Sam, who nodded, confirming her understanding of Andromeda's reference to Earth's moon. Joan felt relief at first. Two months seemed long compared to not knowing if Leo was alive at all. Knowing how much time Leo had was useful, but she still didn't know what to do, or if anything could be done for her brother. The breath of relief was replaced by the same sense of urgency she had felt since Leo was taken. She did not want to wait two months, or two weeks, or two days, or two hours to save her brother. She wanted to save him now.

"Shall we?" said Andromeda.

He stepped aside, gesturing to a sandy path that led up to the entrance of the prison. Andromeda led, followed by Sam, then Joan. The black sand crunched loudly under their feet. Joan felt strange as they approached the Scant prison. Part of her was afraid of so many creatures, like the one that had taken her brother, all being in one place. Andromeda's presence and the light that followed him reassured her.

She had wondered what Sam had meant on Tourlitis when he told them there had been an arrival on Portum Lux just before theirs. She knew now that Sam was referring to a captured Scant brought to the Isle of Mouro to be kept as a prisoner. They reached the entrance, which looked tiny compared to the high walls of the prison. Joan paused as Andromeda and Sam opened and walked through a large steel door. Andromeda and Sam paused as well, looking back at Joan as they held the door open.

"Sam, is there hope? You've both said the Aphotic is unreachable and that no Celestial has ever been rescued. If that's the case, why are we here?" said Joan.

"Never mind what's never happened. In my travels, I have seen the amazing and the unthinkable. If no one's been saved from the Aphotic, then it just hasn't been figured out yet. I believe the secrets of the Aphotic lie with those who know the Aphotic. That's why we are here. To speak with someone who knows the Aphotic," said Sam.

Joan remained still, her eyes studying Sam. "You say there's been a new arrival here. I'm assuming a new Scant has been captured and taken prisoner. If this place is full of Scants, then have they not all been spoken with regarding the Aphotic? Why would a newly captured Scant have anything new to offer."

Sam started to respond, but Andromeda cut him off.

"Sam has brought you here, not because there is a new prisoner, but because that new prisoner knows the Aphotic better than most. One of Dark's elite beings, known as a Light Reaper, is now in our custody. Light Reapers are the most sordid and powerful of Scants. They are very rare and have not been seen in the universe since Dark's defeat in The Nebula Encounters. The Light Reaper was caught, somewhat haphazardly, slinking around a young galaxy. A group of Quasars and Arcs discovered the Scant and, after a short battle, succeeded in capturing the Light Reaper and bringing it here," said Andromeda.

"I see. Do you think this Light Reaper will reveal to us a way to reach the Aphotic and save Leo?" said Joan.

"I do not. The capture of a Light Reaper is rare, and if any being knows the secrets of the Aphotic, it would be a Light Reaper. For that reason, I understand Sam's reasoning for bringing you here to question the new prisoner. However, in the history of Light and Dark, dating back to the beginning of the Nebula Encounters, many have sought ways into the Aphotic, and all have failed. This includes leveraging and torturing captured Scants to find answers. All efforts have failed. Even if our newly captured Light Reaper knows of a way for someone other than a Scant to travel to the Aphotic, I do not believe the Light Reaper will reveal it. Light Reapers are the most knowledgeable of all Scants when it comes to the Aphotic, but they are also the most loyal to, and in love with, Dark," said Andromeda.

"I understand," said Joan.

Sam and Andromeda had revealed to her there was little to no hope. The little amount of hope she did have lay within the mind of a Light Reaper, the highest order of Scant. Her attention moved from the Light Reaper to Leo. Leo's need for her consumed her, and she resolved to hold on to the little hope she had left. Looking between Sam and Andromeda, Joan began nodding her head in determination.

"Take me to the Light Reaper," said Joan.

"Good form, Joan! You heard her, Andromeda, lead her to the Light Reaper," said Sam.

With that, the three of them entered the prison. The floors, walls, and ceilings of the prison were the same black stone as the exterior. A current of light flooded the prison, but not from any visible source. They traveled through cell blocks, passing great sets of stairs that connected the various levels, and by dark rooms, which were seemingly empty. As they walked, Andromeda softly spoke, explaining to Sam and Joan the prison's design and intended effect on its inhabitants.

Andromeda's deep voice, though quiet, echoed through the silent prison as he told Sam and Joan how the prison had two purposes. The first purpose of the prison was to break the connection between Scants and Dark, disarming the Scants' source of power and allowing them to be imprisoned indefinitely. The second purpose of the prison was to reform Scants that had yet to be fully consumed by the desires of Dark. Andromeda described how younger Scants, if separated from Dark long enough, would begin to gravitate toward and embrace the light flowing through the prison. In rare cases, this cultivation from dark to light could result in an imprisoned Scant returning to its former self, before it ever knew Dark. The younger a Scant was when first drawn to Dark, the slimmer the odds of that Scant's reform, as its being would have little to no memory of how to exist without Dark.

As Andromeda continued to lead Sam and Joan through the black halls, the only discernible sounds were their footsteps and Andromeda's voice, as he imparted more knowledge of the prison.

Joan stuck close to Andromeda, peering in each cell they passed. She viewed each cell with a mixture of feelings, like the mixture of light and dark in the air around her. While privately hoping to catch a glimpse of a captured Scant, she also feared what she might see. Though it was impossible to tell which cells were empty and which cells were not, she was weary of each and imagined that every single one contained a Scant sulking in the corner, crouching to avoid the swirling light.

Again, unable to locate a source for the swirling light around her, Joan asked Andromeda where it was coming from. Andromeda took the question in stride, answering as his long steps slowly led them through long dark halls. He explained how the light in the prison came from Quasars, whose galaxies provided a constant stream of light to Portum Lux. Upon entering Portum Lux, Andromeda drew the light to the Isle of Mouro, directing it to fill the prison as he saw fit. It was through this distribution of light that Andromeda, alone, controlled the prison. This made Andromeda, less the thousands of imprisoned Scants, the soul inhabitant of Mouro. Andromeda's status as a Quasar put him in constant communication with the light of Mouro, permitting him to know what was happening in every inch of the prison at any moment in time. This power of light made Andromeda an omniscient steward of the imprisoned Scants, without the need of guards or alarms. When a Scant attempted anything, beyond the will of Andromeda, the light of the prison simply intensified around the Scant until the Scant was paralyzed. Andromeda finished by pointing out that none of the cell doors were locked, because there was no need for locks when you had light.

Joan reacted to this with a quick breath as she began eying the latches of the cells, now realizing that the entire time she had been walking by them they had been unlocked. It made her uneasy, but she took comfort in the presence of Andromeda. She trusted the current of light flowing around her would do as Andromeda had described, keeping the captured Scants just that, captive.

After snaking their way from hall to hall, up and down multiple levels, and through countless wings of cell blocks, they entered a small passageway. At the end of the passageway were two sets of stairs, one to the left and one to the right. Each stair had a shallow slope upward. From the bottom, one couldn't see where either set of stairs finished, just the gradual rise of stone steps, which faded to black like a tunnel.

Andromeda took a step toward the stairs on the left.

"Before you meet the Light Reaper, there's something I need to show you," said Andromeda.

With that, Andromeda began leading Joan up the stairs on their left. As Joan started to climb the stairs, she noticed Sam stayed behind.

"Aren't you coming?" said Joan.

"No. I'll wait here for you to get back. I've been up those stairs enough; no need for me to see it again," said Sam.

"Okay," Joan said hesitantly.

She was unsure of what to make of Sam's comment. Joan had found comfort in Sam's company, and his absence for a part of their journey had not occurred to her. She quickly let it go and continued up the stairs behind Andromeda.

As they made their way up, a bright light came into view at the top. At first distant and small, the light gradually filled more of the stairwell as they climbed. Eventually, the light showed through the cracks around a door at the top of the stairs. At last they reached the door. Joan felt certain they had climbed quite high.

"You should shield your face. Once inside, it will take your eyes a few minutes to adjust," said Andromeda.

Joan nodded her head in acknowledgement and raised an arm across her face, squinting her eyes just wide enough to see where she was going. Andromeda opened the door and they stepped inside.

They were now in the Great Chamber of Mouro. The Great Chamber was expansive and full of light. Crystal covered the entirety of the vaulted space, the floors, the walls, and the ceiling. Everything appeared white and blinding to the eye. Far above, in the center of the chamber, hung a large gem cut in the shape of a globe. The globe and crystal enclosure of the chamber acted as mirrors, causing the light of the room to bounce around endlessly. The infinite rays could not find a surface to be absorbed into.

The rays gave the strangest illusion of, sporadically, changing pace. In one moment, the light would bounce across the room like a herd of shooting stars, while in the next moment, the light slowed and fell like rain. The effect, though beautiful, was overwhelming to the eye. It was impossible to perceive the depth and size of the Great Chamber with the distraction of the infinite rays. One couldn't tell if the chamber's walls were fixed, expanding, or contracting.

After a few minutes, Joan's eyes adjusted enough to where, though still squinting and shielding her eyes, she could behold the Great Chamber. She gazed across the large white space and focused on the globe. It hung far away at the center. Straining her eyes, she began to make out something else in the chamber. Looking up at Andromeda and then back across the chamber, Joan pointed to what looked to be tiny slivers interrupting the white expanse.

"What are those?" said Joan.

"The Veils of Scants," said Andromeda.

Andromeda began striding into the open space of the chamber. Joan followed in awe. Andromeda spoke as they walked.

"This is the Great Chamber of Mouro, where the Veils of captured Scants are forever kept. In this room, each Veil is severed from the power of darkness, unable to link with its Scant. Created long ago, the chamber contains a perpetual light, which was placed in it following its inception. The crystal membrane and the globe were designed to forever reflect the light of the chamber. With no surface to die into, the light will fill this space forever, leaving no room for darkness. It is this echo of light which keeps the Veils, and the Scants of Mouro, at bay."

As they moved farther into the chamber, the tiny slivers grew larger, revealing various profiles of black fabric. The number of Veils in the chamber was countless. Stretched and taut, each Veil was suspended in the air and oriented toward the chamber's globe. Drawing closer to a suspended Veil, Joan could see the black fabric quivering under the light, which had it pinned.

Joan strolled through the Great Chamber of Mouro. It was as if she were walking through a beautiful gallery filled with horrific art; she was both enthralled and terrified. When she neared the center of the chamber, her eyes were drawn to the globe. As she circled it, she was mesmerized by its beauty and purity, and found it difficult to look away. Like the Veils, she was captivated by the globe's light. Unlike the Veils, however, she enjoyed it.

As she continued to circle the globe, Joan unknowingly approached a suspended Veil. She drew closer and closer to the unseen Veil, her eyes still focused on the globe above. The hair on her neck stood as she sensed an imminent collision. She jerked her eyes from the globe and turned to brace herself for contact. Once turned, she found herself staring into darkness. Her face was a few inches from the stretched fabric of the Veil. The Veil seemed to jump at the prospect of touching Joan, though the pinned Veil was unable to stretch the last few inches and embrace her.

With short breaths, Joan took a step back from the Veil. The outstretched fabric spanned like an enormous black shroud in front of her. This Veil was larger than the others in the chamber and could have wrapped Joan fifty times over. Not only was this Veil the largest in the chamber, it was the closest to the globe. While the other Veils in the chamber quivered under the light, this Veil shook violently against it.

Andromeda had been observing Joan. He walked alongside her and placed his hand on her shoulder. He pulled her a few steps farther back from the menacing Veil. Now at a safe distance, they observed in silence the behemoth before them.

The large Veil seemed to stare back at them, continuing to shudder under the light. The longer they stood there, the angrier the Veil seemed to get, as if being antagonized by the Quasar and

Arc. The Veil started to writhe and shake viciously, determined to break free from its bondage. Summoning a final gasp, the Veil, fueled by hate for the two beings standing before it, unleashed a thrash violent enough to cause its fabric to release a piercing scream from the pressure. Joan covered her ears and looked away, while Andromeda stoically watched the suffering Veil. Shackled and defeated by the Great Chamber, the Veil subsided.

"Why is it like that? Why isn't it like the others?" said Joan.

"That Veil doesn't belong to a normal Scant. It belongs to a Light Reaper," said Andromeda.

"*My* Light Reaper?" said Joan.

"Yes," said Andromeda.

They walked back across the white expanse, toward where they had entered. Joan's mind was consumed by the Veil of the Light Reaper. She felt the Veil's desire for her as she walked among the infinite rays. The chamber's light continued its shifting appearance from shooting stars to rain, and back again. They exited the Great Chamber of Mouro and made the long descent down. Once reaching the bottom of the stairs, they found Sam where they had left him, leaning against the black stone wall of the passageway and sleeping while standing up. Andromeda gave a cough and Sam came to, his mustache bobbing like a seesaw as he cleared his throat and struggled to wake up.

"Well ... " growled Sam. "I'm sure glad I didn't go with you. That damn room gives me the creeps. It's a wonder they don't call it the 'Damned Chamber' instead of the 'Great Chamber.'"

Joan smiled; she was happy to be with Sam again. They hadn't been apart for long, but she had missed the contrast he provided in the prison. She turned her attention to the other set of stairs before them, which mirrored those to the Great Chamber.

"Are you ready to see the Light Reaper?" said Andromeda.

"Yes," said Joan.

She was nervous as they began the ascent up the second set of stairs. Joan wrestled with the prospect of facing the Light Reaper. The only Scant she had come face to face with had taken Leo from her. If she couldn't face a Scant then, how could she expect to face a member of Dark's highest order, especially after seeing the Light Reaper's Veil in the chamber? Joan imagined the Light Reaper being as large and vicious as its veil. She was terrified. However, even worse than the thought of facing the Light Reaper was the thought of facing the Light Reaper and not discovering a way to save Leo.

"Sam. What if we can't get anything from the Light Reaper? Or what if there's nothing to get? What if there is no secret that will lead us to Leo, and this is all for nothing?" said Joan.

"Joan. You must have faith. What else is there but to believe? The knowledge and secrets of the Aphotic lie with the Light Reapers. The question is not whether there's a way to the Aphotic. The question is whether we can extract the secrets from the Light Reaper. When dealing with the Light Reaper, we must be patient. Your brother has two months, so if we are unsuccessful today, we will try again tomorrow. If necessary, we will interrogate the Light Reaper every hour of every day while your brother still has hope," said Sam.

"How will we interrogate the Light Reaper? Do you have a strategy in mind?" said Joan.

"Yes, I have a strategy in mind," said Sam.

"That's great! What is it? How do you plan to approach the Light Reaper?" said Joan.

"I don't plan to approach the Light Reaper at all. That will be your job," said Sam.

Joan was not expecting this. She went silent for a few moments as they continued up the stairs toward the Light Reaper's cell.

"What do you mean, my job? You don't expect me to face the Light Reaper alone, do you?" said Joan.

"Actually, I do. You facing the Light Reaper alone is the best chance we have," said Sam.

"That's insane. How am I supposed to know what to say or what to do? There's nothing I can offer, no line of questioning or tact I can imagine that would result in the Light Reaper revealing anything to me. Why would the Light Reaper ever give me secrets about the Aphotic? Especially if it knows I'm seeking a way to save my Celestial brother?"

They reached a landing at the top of the stairs. There was a door that looked like the one to the Great Chamber, but there was no light coming through the cracks. It was the Light Reaper's cell.

"You'll just have to trust me, I guess," said Sam.

"No. I'm not going in there alone unless you explain yourself. Why me instead of you or Andromeda? Your knowledge would be an asset in speaking with the Light Reaper, while Andromeda's force could compel the Light Reaper to cooperate. I have neither your mind nor Andromeda's power. So why me?" said Joan.

"Neither my mind, nor Andromeda's power, will affect the Light Reaper. We know this from experience with lesser Scants, and we can't waste time on tactics proven to fail. My hope is that, with this particular Light Reaper, your presence will bring a new tactic. Something different than knowledge or force," said Sam.

"And what is that?" said Joan, looking up at Andromeda and Sam, who stood between her and the door to the Light Reaper's cell.

"That she sees some of herself in you," said Andromeda.

"*She*?" said Joan.

Joan was caught off guard. It hadn't occurred to her the Light Reaper could be a woman.

"Yes. Her name is Sordara. She is truly one of the darkest creatures in creation, and worthy of her status as a Light Reaper," said Andromeda.

The Quasar turned toward the cell. The swirling light of the prison obeyed Andromeda and released the cell door, allowing it to swing open. Joan steadied herself, taking a few slow breaths to rule her nerve, and stepped inside, coming face to face with Sordara.

CHAPTER EIGHT
ECLAIREUR

Ko stepped off the empty ship. He had reached the Isle of Eclaireur. While wondering about Aileen's and Joan's journeys, he was also on guard for what was to come next. His eyes darted around, surveying his surroundings.

Flanked by water on all sides, Ko was once again standing on a small island. This island differed from Tourlitis. Instead of looking out across an empty ocean, he was looking across a bay, which died into a large mainland. It belonged to the Isle of Eclaireur.

Like Tourlitis, the small island on which Ko stood supported a free-standing lighthouse. The structure of the Eclaireur lighthouse was built of stone. The bottom third of its exterior was painted red, the middle third painted white, and red again for the top third. A black pinnacle, with a glass enclosure like that of the Tourlitis lighthouse, capped the structure. The pinnacle of the Eclaireur lighthouse received the signal that had been sent by Sam on Tourlitis. The unmanned ship on which Ko had arrived was the response to this signal.

As far as Ko could see in each direction, the mainland of Eclaireur was walled by white capped mountains. The mountains stood tall and resolute, protecting what lay beyond, as if by design. The air was cold. He hugged himself as he examined what was now a dusk-like atmosphere filling the sky. A fading daylight was giving way to starlight, though the stars of Portum Lux provided a starlight so bright that the day was unable to fully reach night.

"Yes, lad," a voice said.

Ko turned to find a man standing nearby. The man was speaking to Ko.

"Um, hi," said Ko.

"Me name is Grubb. What are ye called?"

"I'm Ko. I didn't see you here when I arrived. Where did you come from? Do you know Sam?"

Ko eyed Grubb cautiously.

"There ain't no time fer silly questions. Ye know how I got here an' o' course I knows Sam. I figgered maybe ye'd be smart. Maybe I was wrong," said Grubb.

Grubb's dialect was thick, and he had the appearance to match. He looked like a man who was always ready to fight. He was broad and athletic, with a thick blond beard, ragged blond hair, and a burly face. He wore thick canvas pants and a matching sweater. The material was tan and rugged, designed for warmth and taking a beating. A hood fell from the back of the sweater and hung down Grubb's back. The neckline of the sweater was cut in a V-shape and had crisscrossing ties that could be cinched or loosened. The ensemble was completed by a pair of coarse gray leather boots.

"No worries, lad. Not ever'body can be smart. I say, better to have a little sperit than to have a heap o' smart. So, what about sperit, do ye have it?"

Ko ignored Grubb's insults and settled into the banter.

"Sure, I have spirit," said Ko.

"That's good, ye're gonna need sperit. It's quare cold out here an' ye look wrecked. What say ye about gettin' out o' here, an' findin' ye some warmer clothes?"

Ko nodded his head, still hugging himself against the cold. Grubb walked toward Ko, grabbed him by the arm, and they warped deep into the mountains of Eclaireur.

Ko found himself standing in a dark cavern. He was underground and surrounded by a different kind of cold. Light twinkled from torch-like devices fastened to the walls and ceiling of the large cave-like space. Leveled and polished, the floor was even and smooth, whereas the walls and ceilings had been left rocky and untouched. Randomly throughout the large void, columns had been added to support beams and trusses, which shored the raw rock of the cavern. The shoring columns were made of petrified timber and glistened with the light.

Filling the floor space of the cavern were beds, lots of beds. The empty beds were alone in the room, except for Ko and Grubb. Waiting for Ko on one of the beds was a change of clothes matching what Grubb wore. Ko pulled on the canvas pants, hooded sweater, and gray boots. The new threads provided much needed warmth, which he welcomed.

"Where are we?" said Ko.

"We're in a mountain known as the Alveare o' Eclaireur, the great stronghold o' Arcs across the universe, where Arcs like ye an' me get fit to face the nastiest creatures this side o' the whole shebang," said Grubb.

Grubb's parlance contained a hint of pride and daring in his answer.

"I see, and why are all of these beds here?" said Ko.

"The cavern ye're in, an' all the beds ye see, are fer young Arcs, green ones. It's called the Green Cavern. This is where ye'll be stayin' durin' ye're time on Eclaireur. Ye know, because ye're green."

"I guess that makes sense," said Ko.

Content with his explanation of where they were, Grubb walked toward one end of the cavern, and Ko followed. They exited through a door cut in the rock and entered a tunnel, offering two directions for them to choose from.

"Follow me an' I'll show ye the rest o' the grounds," said Grubb.

Grubb started walking left down the tunnel. Ko followed. They passed doors and other tunnels, which every now and then Grubb would silently enter or turn down. Ko struggled to track their direction. He couldn't tell if they were going up, down, forward, or doubling back. It felt as if they were moving through a large ant mound.

Like the Green Cavern, light in the tunnels came from torch-like devices fastened to the walls. They weren't torches though. The light didn't appear to come from a flame. It was just there, hovering above the tops of the torches.

They silently covered great distance before entering a final tunnel, which dead-ended with a pair of large doors. Grubb pushed through the doors and out into a vast clearing. The clearing sprung from the base of the mountain, a great release from the Alveare.

Coated with coarse sand, the clearing revealed itself to be a sprawling courtyard of sorts. The courtyard was bracketed by large mountains on three sides, with the far end of the courtyard, directly in front of them, offering a more open view. The view contained a beautiful lake contained by far off mountains. Looking down on the lake and the courtyard from the sky would show that together they formed an oval, walled by skyscraping peaks along the oval's perimeter. The oval could only be accessed by warping or parachuting in, as there were no paths from the Portum Lux seas through the mountains.

They walked away from the base of the Alveare and toward the lake. A brisk breeze moved against them from the lake. The crude canvas fabric around their bodies cut the cold as they walked. After a few hundred meters or so, they reached the middle of the courtyard. Turning back and facing the direction from which they had come, Grubb pointed back to the Alveare.

"There's much in the mountain. Everythin' from libraries to mess halls, observatories to mines, an' much more. With time, ye'll come to learn the mountain. Fer the ferseeable future, all ye need to know is where to sleep, where to eat, an' where to train. Ye've seen where ye sleep. I'll show ye later where to eat. What ye see here,"—Grubb motioned around at the courtyard—"is where ye'll train."

Ko surveyed the empty grounds. "Where is everyone?"

"It's just ye an' me. We get a few stragglers, from time to time, who are lookin' to train an' master the craft, but since the Nebula Encounters were won, there's been fewer an' fewer Arcs comin' through here. The Dark lost its teeth after most Scants were vanquished or captured. Fer a long time now, Arcs an' their Celestials have been mostly safe. Arcs haven't needed bendin' time to protect Celestials. Back when Scants were snatchin' Nebulas, this place was buzzin' with Arcs, all trainin' an' masterin' the grit it takes to face a Scant. An' grit is what it takes. Scants are nasty creatures."

Nostalgically, Grubb scanned the empty grounds.

Ko was amazed that a mountain and space so large could only have one inhabitant. "Why are you here?" he said.

"I'm steward o' the Alveare. I'm here to look after everythin' an', from time to time, train Arcs who are lookin' fer grit. An' I know what ye're next question is gonna be: me Celestial is fine. Me sister reached Quasar an' is off with Light, safe in the universe."

"That's good," said Ko.

Ko was sincere in his response, as he thought of Aileen. He knew she was safe for now, but he longed for her to become like Grubb's sister. To reach a place where she would forever be out of harm's way.

Grubb saw what Ko was thinking.

"What's yer Celestial's name?" said Grubb.

"Aileen."

"Ah, a sister. I know what ye're feelin'. Mark me, if ye do as I says, we'll make ye the meanest Arc this side o' the Aphotic, fit to do anythin' an' everythin' necessary to protect her from the nasties."

"That sounds good to me," said Ko.

He appreciated Grubb's sentiment, though he wondered how long his training would take.

"How long will it take before I'm the meanest Arc this side of the Aphotic?" asked Ko.

"That, lad, depends entirely on ye. There is no set time for an Arc's trainin', though the best pick it up quick."

Ko nodded his head in understanding and let his attention drift to the lake. Smooth and polished, the lake's surface acted as a mirror of the landscape. Periodically, a gust of wind would cause the lake's reflection of the mountains and sky to shudder. While admiring the mirror effect, something caught his eye across the water. A shift in the distance had interrupted the still landscape. He began walking toward the lake. The movement came into focus when he reached the shore.

A still object protruded from the center of the lake. What had caught Ko's eye was something moving around the object, above the water's surface. Fear gripped him as he recognized the black fabric, shapelessly hovering above the lake. Grubb had silently followed Ko to the water's edge and now stood just off Ko's shoulder.

"Grubb, a Scant."

Ko's voice was earnest, his eyes locked on the Veil. His fists tightened as he prepared for what might happen next.

"No, lad, not exactly," said Grubb.

Grubb's tone didn't reveal fear or concern. Confused, Ko looked at Grubb.

"I don't understand. That's a Scant's Veil, right?" said Ko.

He pointed to the Veil and continued to scan the area for an accompanying Scant.

"It's a Scant's Veil, all right, but the Scant to which it belongs is not here," said Grubb.

Grubb's answer relaxed Ko, though he remained confused.

"Why is the Veil here?" Ko asked.

"There's somethin' at the center o' the lake the Veil protects," said Grubb.

"What does it protect?" said Ko.

Grubb motioned toward the object protruding out of the center of the lake, around which the Veil hovered. The object was a granite podium rising from the water. Sitting on top of the podium was a small wooden chest.

"It's protectin' what's in that chest," said Grubb.

Ko focused on the top of the granite podium. The wood of the small chest stood out against the gray backdrop of the mountains.

"What's in the chest?" said Ko.

"The eyes o' a Scant," said Grubb.

Grubb's answer filled Ko with dread. At once he understood. A Scant had been defeated and its eyes removed to produce the scenario that he now observed. While the Scant was no more, its Veil remained innocently loyal to what remained of its former master. The eyes of the defeated Scant now rested at the center of the lake for all to see, eternally watched by the departed Scant's Veil. Ko recognized the cruelness of the trick and the relativity of cruelness. He didn't feel bad for the dead Scant or the fooled Veil. The dread he had felt initially faded into a feeling of awareness. Awareness that savagery could exist on either side of good versus evil.

Ko knew there was a reason behind the savagery he was taking in.

"Why did they do that? You know, put the eyes out there like that?" said Ko.

"It's a test intended to simulate facin' a Scant, an' its reserved fer the bravest an' most capable Arcs. Any Arc who succeeds in stealin' the eyes without the Veil gettin' 'em is deemed Arc-Iris, the highest order o' Arc," said Grubb.

"Are you Arc-Iris?" said Ko.

"Mmm-hmm," responded Grubb nodding his head up and down. "But I ain't ever tried to steal the eyes out from under that Veil there." Grubb motioned again towards the center of the lake. "I became Arc-Iris out in the mess they call creation. Chasin' down Scants an' goin' head to head with 'em, fortunate to come out the other side. Becomin' Arc-Iris can occur here on Eclaireur by gettin' them eyes, or by facin' a real life Scant an' puttin' em down."

"How many have succeeded?" said Ko.

"Very few. Whether it be tryin' to steal the eyes from this lake or facin' a Scant out in the mess, not many Arcs have done it. It's a tall task. Ye need not get any ideas either. Ye're a far cry from thinkin' bout tryin' that Veil out there. Ye need to focus on crawlin' befer thinkin' bout runnin'."

With that they left the lake and its Veil behind, intent on finding food and rest in preparation for Ko's training to begin the next day. They entered the Alveare through the same doors from before. Grubb toured Ko around various passageways, pointing down dark fissures and up vertical tunnels, describing the various chambers and rooms to which they led. Eventually, they found a kitchen galley where Grubb prepared two heaping plates of hash, eggs, and sausage. Once prepped, they carried the steaming plates through a short tunnel and into a large cavity of the mountain. The cavity was a mess hall, filled with long rows of empty tables.

Each bite and clatter of silverware echoed through the empty space. Ko was ravenous for food, so he was content to eat while Grubb told stories and illustrated with his hands what it was like when the rows of tables had been full of thousands of Arcs breaking bread together. After Ko had his fill of food and stories, they cleaned up and left to find their beds. Grubb disappeared into one room while Ko walked the tunnels until he located the Green Cavern once again and found his bed.

Lying down, Ko stared at the rocky ceiling far above. The Veil of the lake looped through his mind. He had been fighting a nameless urge since seeing the Veil and learning about the eyes that it protected. Ko knew what was in the chest at the center of the lake, but knowing wasn't enough for him. He wanted to see the eyes for himself. Drifting to sleep, he dreamed about the silent Veil floating nearby, ready to dart and consume anyone who approached.

In the morning, Ko received his first instruction. Standing in the cold of the courtyard, he sought to follow Grubb's direction. Grubb explained how an Arc's mind could do more than perceive time, and that the ability to communicate with time lay within Ko.

"Arcs communicatin' with time is like a bein' interactin' with another bein'," started Grubb. "A relationship. That's what it is. The stronger the relation, the clearer the dialogue, the greater the potential. Like all relations, it must be initiated by one party. In yer case, as it is with all Arcs, time initiates the relationship by simply makin' itself available to the Arc."

Grubb proceeded to warp around the courtyard, disappearing and appearing in various locations, covering the distances instantly. Ko watched longingly, wanting very badly to learn the art. While he knew warping was a serious matter for the protection of Aileen, he couldn't help but think of how fun it looked. Returning to Ko's side, Grubb picked up where he had left off.

"What ye just observed is possible because time in the universe is linear, with a single moment coverin' the entirety o' existence an' space. What this means, young Arc, is that a moment at one end o' the universe is the same moment occurin' on the opposite side o' the universe. An Arc need only acknowledge this truth, specific to his location an' where he desires to go. Once acknowledged, time creates the opportunity fer a step from one location, across vast distances, to the other location, all within the same moment o' time that exists in both locations."

Ko's head spun as Grubb directed him to focus on a far-off spot in the courtyard and to acknowledge a moment of time that existed in the far-off spot as well as where Ko stood. Ko focused and gave the far-off spot his attention. He sought to force the spot to be within stepping distance, as if telling the distance that it wasn't real. Straining his mind caused his body to tense and lean forward in anticipation. Nothing happened. The distance was real.

The harder Ko tried, the more impossible it seemed to create a fantasy connection allowing him to step past distance and through time. Unsure of how to use his mind and body to warp, hours began to pass without him doing more than exerting random thoughts and steps in the same spot he had started in. Grubb looked on silently, showing no emotion or urgency regarding Ko's inability to warp.

Ko's focus began to fade. His thoughts, more and more, found their way back to Aileen. What if he was unable to become a true Arc, and incapable of truly protecting the one he cared about most? Exasperated, and no longer able to focus on the far-off spot, he gave up.

Ko shot a dejected glance in Grubb's direction before tilting his head back and staring at the sky of Portum Lux. He thought to himself, at least Aileen is safe on Portum Lux, where real Arcs, like Grubb, can protect her. This thought, and the beauty of the Portum Lux sky brought a calm upon him. Relaxed, he pulled his gaze down and looked again to the far-off spot he had been staring at all day. He thought he saw something, and he decided to walk across the courtyard for a closer look.

After taking a step forward, Ko turned to look at Grubb, but Grubb wasn't there. Quickly, he glanced around at his surroundings to find Grubb was standing off in the distance. Ko assumed Grubb had warped to the other side of the courtyard. However, as Ko's surroundings came into focus, he realized that he was the one who had warped. Ko had stepped across the courtyard, to the far-off spot he had desired, covering a distance in one step, which should have taken many steps.

The young Arc felt the kind of joy anyone feels when they do something they didn't know they were capable of. Grubb warped across the courtyard, appearing right next to Ko and putting his arm around him. Grubb wore an intense smile matching how his student felt. The ability within Ko had been released. He embraced Grubb and yelled in triumph, his voice sounding across the valley and against the mountains.

As his excitement faded, Ko felt an exhaustion come over him. Seeing the turn in the boy, Grubb explained that the physical toll from warping would be draining, but with time, his mind and body would build an endurance against the toll. Ko nodded in understanding, too weak to speak. Grubb warped them back to the Green Cavern, where Ko fell asleep immediately on his bed.

The next day, Ko woke, famished for food. Making his way to the kitchen galley, he found a grand breakfast prepared by Grubb. He inhaled the meal as Grubb observed silently. Upon finishing the breakfast, Ko felt reenergized. He was excited to visit the courtyard. The thrill of warping, of covering distance instantly, of overcoming physics, was an experience he was eager to have again.

Grubb and Ko exited the mountain and entered the courtyard to begin the second day of training. Grubb picked up where he had left off the day before, addressing the exhaustion Ko had felt after warping.

Grubb explained how each Arc responded differently to bending time, and that the greatest Arcs could endure many instances of bending time, consecutively, without experiencing fatigue. Grubb elaborated further, describing how an Arc's endurance, as in the number of times an Arc can bend time without failing due to exhaustion, was a function of the Arc's conditioning, natural ability, and determination.

Ko nodded. He resolved to take care of what he could control, and that was determination.

☀ ☀ ☀

Days passed as Ko warped around the grounds, with each warp being a challenge set forth by Grubb, harder than the one before. Eventually, the challenge of great distances, combined with the inability to see the destination, was taken on by Ko as he stretched the breadth of his imagination and ability.

Grubb followed Ko around the grounds with each warp, staying right behind him. It became apparent to Grubb that warping came easier to Ko than other Arcs, with the relationship of time from one location to another becoming effortless for Ko to connect. Grubb didn't reveal this observation to Ko. Instead, he allowed the boy to push himself further and further against the bounds of time without knowing he was performing well. Eventually, Ko was warping from mountain peak to mountain peak, throughout Eclaireur, with Grubb working hard to keep up. Grubb decided that Ko was ready for more than just warping.

One day, after many spent warping, Ko awoke, had a quick stack of pancakes with sausages in the galley, and made his way to the courtyard, eager for more. Entering the courtyard alone, Ko waited for Grubb to appear. A few minutes passed, but he saw no sign of him. An hour passed and still no sign. The morning passed, and the afternoon came with no sign of Grubb. Ko paced back and forth in the courtyard, unsure of what to do without his instructor. With Grubb absent, Ko passed the time watching the black silhouette of the lake's Veil. Far off, it shifted above the glassy water.

After the daylight had nearly faded, the harsh voice Ko had come to know well cut the silence of the courtyard.

"Figgered I was some 'where else, aye?"

Grubb's voice sounded a few feet away from Ko. The boy smiled, relieved to hear Grubb's voice. Grubb removed the obscure he had created, revealing himself, and asked Ko if he was ready to graduate from warping and move on to the craft of obscuring. Ko, in a manner undramatic, yet serious, nodded yes.

Ko's training in the craft of creating an obscure, like his training in warping, began with an overture from Grubb on the mechanics behind an Arc communicating with time. Like warping, the art of obscuring began with acknowledging the truth of time being linear, with the same moment spreading across all of creation. Whereas acknowledging this truth in warping allowed an Arc to connect one location to another for travel, acknowledging this truth in obscuring allowed an Arc to connect several locations to one another for cloaking oneself as invisible. Grubb went on to explain how obscuring demanded a different imagination and greater ability from an Arc than warping.

The first level of obscuring, he explained, required an Arc to bend a moment of time across several locations for an instant. Such a feat causes an Arc to simply disappear for a split second before reappearing. Though not very useful, it is considered more difficult for an Arc to achieve than warping.

The second level of obscuring challenged an Arc to create several bends of time in the same moment while maintaining the multitude of connections from moment to moment, allowing the Arc to remain cloaked and invisible. Accomplishing this allows the Arc to remain invisible, but only if the Arc remains perfectly still, Grubb warned.

The third level, reserved for the most advanced of Arcs, demanded the skill to maintain the cloak of an obscure while moving. For an Arc to move within an obscure, cloaked, he or she must constantly recreate the connections that shield the Arc. For most Arcs, the third level of obscuring is never achieved.

Over the course of a few days, Ko and Grubb worked in the courtyard without rest as Ko tried his hand at obscuring. His first task from Grubb was to accomplish the first level of obscuring, creating multiple connections around his immediate person within the same moment.

The young Arc did not manage well with his new task. Though he spent every waking hour at it, day after day, he only managed to achieve a handful of brief connections, resulting in his body being partially cloaked for an instant. Though not impressive, the effort to create these split-second obscures took a toll on Ko. Like his first experience with warping, he often needed rest and food to reenergize after each session.

Whereas Grubb had been pleased with Ko's ability to warp, he quickly became impatient with his student's lack of progress in obscuring. One afternoon, he sought to jog the boy's imagination in the matter.

"Vectors an' points! Vectors an' points! Get out o' yer head, lad. All aroun' yer body, across every dimension o' the space aroun' ye, exists but one moment! The space is different. The points aroun' ye are different, but they all have the same moment in common. Understan' that, if divided up small enough, the number o' points aroun' yer person is infinite. Understan', yer mind can't go one by one an' contemplate an infinite number o' points! So, quit tryin'! Instead, simply recognize that the space aroun' ye shares one moment, an' through that moment ask the infinite group o' vectors, an' points, an' space aroun' ye to swap!"

Ko struggled to follow Grubb's instruction. Frustrated with his failure, and with Grubb's rambling logic, he resolved that the heart of Grubb's instruction was to not try so hard.

Ko relaxed. He let go of trying to identify and control every point in space around him, and instead focused on the singularity of a moment. From there he sought to initiate a request, instead of a directive, to the collective points of space surrounding him. For a moment, the space around him responded, and for that moment, a fully connected obscure was created around his body, creating the allusion that he was not standing where he was.

"Yes, lad!" said Grubb as the obscure flashed around Ko's body, causing the young Arc to fully disappear for a split second.

"It worked?" asked Ko.

"It did indeed. No time to bask now; do it again but hold on to it. An entire day needs to pass with ye in an obscure, unmovin', an' out o' sight."

Grubb's new task was for Ko to achieve the second level of obscuring. Ko got right to it, pressing himself to create an obscure and maintain it for an entire day. He showed promise with each attempt, disappearing under his obscures and remaining invisible for longer and longer periods of time. Many days passed as he zeroed in on the goal Grubb had set for him.

He came to enjoy his new existence with Grubb on Eclaireur. A routine consumed with training and rest, obscuring and exhaustion, where any time spared between rest and obscuring was spent cooking and eating elaborate breakfasts. Ko had come to love the breakfast food they ate, regardless of what meal it was or time of day. He had accepted that Grubb either only knew how to make breakfast, or that Grubb knew perfectly well how to prepare other meals but just didn't want to. Either way, he was okay with it.

One morning, at the break of dawn, Ko arrived in the courtyard as part of what had become his routine on Eclaireur. He produced an obscure around himself. The morning came and went with Ko remaining invisible. The afternoon passed as well, with no break in the obscure. Grubb stared at the spot where Ko was standing for the entire day, both unmoving. The last part of the day came and went with Ko unseen. Grubb, satisfied with Ko's performance, gave relief to his student.

"Alright, lad, that's enough," said Grubb.

Ko released the obscure and collapsed on the ground, his body exhausted. Starving and dehydrated, he didn't have the energy to get back up. Grubb intervened, warping Ko inside the mountain, where they each inhaled a large omelet. After the meal, they found their beds and slept. Ko slept through the night, and the next day.

Finally waking almost two days later, Ko smelled an aroma of bacon, which had filled the cavern. He found a few pans' worth of French toast and bacon that Grubb had prepared in the galley. Not seeing Grubb around, Ko made a plate of just bacon crisscrossed into a tiny tower and smothered it with syrup. After inhaling the architectural wonder, he made his way back to the courtyard, anxious to try his hand at the third level of obscuring.

As Ko entered the courtyard, he found his mind was unusually clear following the long rest. Further, he felt a confidence he hadn't known previously. He was no longer unsure of himself or what he was capable of. He felt a new desire to not only master what others could do but to seek out and master what others had never attempted. His desire landed on an object he had found himself daydreaming about since he had arrived on Eclaireur—the eyes of the lake. When he wasn't training, or eating, or sleeping, Ko daydreamed about beating the Veil of the lake and looking inside the box it protected. It was a strange urge to which he could not name a source.

Ko's daydreaming, and constant training, had caused him to lose track of time since parting with Joan and Aileen. He wondered how many weeks had passed and found himself guessing, as he started to worry about whether Joan's brother still had time. An urgency settled on him as he waited for Grubb to arrive in the courtyard. Ko had sworn that he would be ready to help Joan save Leo if she found a way. He had to be ready.

Grubb entered the courtyard with energy, pleased with Ko's progress and looking forward to challenging Ko with the third level of obscuring, moving while invisible. Grubb knew from experience how valuable it could be when facing Scants. Though the task was a tall one for any Arc to achieve, Grubb believed that this young Arc was capable.

Grubb approached and prepared to give a long overview of the mechanics behind the third level of obscuring, but he never got the chance.

Before Grubb got a word out, Ko disappeared within an obscure. A minute later, Ko appeared next to, and put his arm around, Grubb.

"I think I've got it," said Ko.

Grubb stood looking at Ko with a bewildered expression, amazed at what he had just seen. The elder Arc let a few wordless seconds pass. He processed Ko's ability to obscure at the highest level with zero instruction. It was apparent to Grubb that Ko's abilities were now fully in sync with time.

Without saying anything, Grubb disappeared from the courtyard. He warped to an armory deep in the Alveare and then back to Ko in the courtyard. Upon returning, Grubb held a few items in his arms. Among the items were two daggers. He handed one of the daggers to Ko.

Ko held the blade up and examined it. The dagger consisted of a hilt made of petrified wood, which gave way to a long slender blade. He turned the dagger from side to side before softly lowering the blade to rest on his skin. Without applying pressure, the blade drew a small amount of blood.

"Fer now, stash that away," said Grubb.

Grubb reached out to hand Ko something else. It was a wooden version of the same dagger. He also handed him a gold sash. Ko watched as Grubb wrapped his own sash around his waist, holstering both the wooden and real dagger within the gold fabric. Ko followed suit.

"Follow me," said Grubb.

Grubb warped across the courtyard to the edge of the lake. Ko followed. They each stared at the eyes of the lake and the on-guard Veil.

"I've seen ye lookin' at the eyes. I can tell ye want to take a run at the Veil. Do ye think ye're ready?" said Grubb.

"I'm not sure. I don't know why I want to see the eyes so badly," said Ko.

"I know what ye mean. Here's the deal. From here on out, from when each day begins to when the day ends, ye an' I are playin' a little game. If ye can beat me at our little game, then ye'll be ready to go after them eyes."

"What game?" said Ko.

"Tag," said Grubb.

Grubb pulled the wooden dagger out of his sash, swiped it across the back of Ko's head, and disappeared into a warp.

Ko rubbed the sting out from the back of his head. With the wooden dagger in his hand, he took one last look at the eyes and its Veil before warping after Grubb, intent on tagging the Arc-Iris.

CHAPTER NINE
SKYE

Aileen stood on the shore of Skye. As far as she could see in each direction, moor-like cliffs blocked her view of what lay inland. She eyed a path cut in the rock and ambled up to it. The path snaked and climbed from the shore to the top of the cliffs. Slowly making her way through the rocks, Aileen left the shore behind and sought to find what lay beyond. In time, she cleared the hike and found herself standing on top of the moor cliffs, looking back down on the shore.

She turned from the sea to behold the highlands of Skye. Basking in light, waves of rolling hills covered with lush grass stretched as far as she could see. Crops of purple thistles and granite mounds scattered the lumpy yet beautiful terrain. Aileen took a deep breath. The air tasted delicious and flooded her senses with a freshness and warmth beyond anything she had ever experienced. It felt as if Skye was giving her a big hug, and she wanted to return the favor.

She strolled though the grass, weaving through pods of blooming thistles, not thinking of where she was going or whether she might meet other Celestials. In this moment, her sole purpose was to enjoy the beauty around her as only a child could.

After walking a ways, Aileen came across a hill that looked inviting for a rest. It rose as a tump of granite splotched with grass and moss. Once atop the hill, Aileen's surmise was confirmed, as she discovered the blend of warmth and breeze perfect for a nap. She found a soft bed of moss and laid herself down, the light of Skye folding around her like a blanket. Though, just as she closed her eyes, she was intruded upon.

"Hello," said the intruder.

Aileen was not panicked, because the intruder's voice was fair. She opened her eyes and sat up to see who the fair voice belonged to. The space around her remained how she had found it, with empty beds of moss among the granite and nobody in sight. She looked in each direction twice to be sure.

"Hello," Aileen said sheepishly.

"Do you know where you are?"

Unsure of whether she was truly awake, Aileen rubbed her eyes and gave her arm a few pinches, as she could still not locate a figure for the voice, which seemed to belong to a mossy boulder only a few paces away.

"Yes, this is Skye. Can I ask where you are? I hear you, but I can't see you," said Aileen, addressing the mossy boulder.

"It is alright for you to ask. I am near, though I am hiding myself."

"Why?" asked Aileen.

"To protect you."

"From what?" asked Aileen, still sitting on her moss bed.

"My face."

"Hmm," started Aileen. "Could you show yourself but hide your face? Or at the very least, reveal a toe so I know where you stand?"

"As you wish."

Aileen stood and observed as the airspace in front of the mossy boulder began to shimmer. A small fissure formed in the nearby atmos, from which slowly sprung a white shadow. It was of mild stature, forming into robe-like garments, and emitting a clear white light that mesmerized Aileen. She could see that the fair voice of the intruder matched its physical nature, a pale translucence balanced with a dazzling brilliance. As promised, the intruder's face remained hidden, recessed in hooded garments that created a tunnel-like effect, from which milky beams flowed.

"Is that better?"

"Yes, thank you," said Aileen, with an absent-minded smile, her senses overwhelmed by the beauty of the white shadow.

"How do you feel?"

"I ... dunno," said Aileen. She thought of her parents, the Scant, of Leo being in the Aphotic and Joan seeking to save him, and of being away from Ko.

"It's okay. You can tell me."

"I feel, um, scared. But I also feel warm. I'm not scared for me. It just feels like something bad could happen," said Aileen.

"Let not your heart be troubled. Sometimes bad things happen. In the end, those things are made right. Do you believe that? That bad things are made right?"

"Yes," said Aileen.

"Good. Do you know what love is?"

"I think so," said Aileen.

"Tell me, then, what is love?"

"Mom always said love is the in-between," said Aileen.

"Like a feeling?"

"No, I don't think so," said Aileen.

"What do you think your mother meant, then, calling love the in-between?"

"I'm not really sure," said Aileen, as she shrugged her shoulders.

"It's okay. Just try."

"Well, my dad said it was like magnets when they're backwards and you try to push them together, but they won't go together," said Aileen.

"So, love is magnetic?"

"No. Love's not magnetic. I think I said it wrong. It's not the pull or the push. It has to do with the space between two magnets when they're backwards, the space the two magnets can't get to because they're pushing away from one another. Love fills that space, the in-between. It goes where other things can't go," said Aileen.

Her voice had lost its sheepish quality. She began to speak with a more reflective and informative tone.

"Oh, I see. Love fills voids, connecting two, which otherwise couldn't be connected?"

"Yep," said Aileen.

"Can you touch love, or do you feel love?"

"Neither. It's somewhere in between," Aileen said, "like a gooey center, you can't know until you're there."

"Well, your mother and father were right about love. It goes where nothing else can go and fills abysses that are unseen. It is truly the in-between."

"I'm afraid my mom and dad are gone," Aileen said quietly, with a sadness seeping into her voice.

"Where do you think they have gone?"

"I dunno; they're just gone," said Aileen.

"Can you reach them?"

"I don't think so," said Aileen.

"What about love? Can love reach them?"

"I hope so," said Aileen.

"Truly, love is the in-between, and your love can go where nothing else can."

"Can my love go where Leo is?" Her voice rose with hope as she asked this question.

"It can."

"Can I go where Leo is, in the Aphotic?" said Aileen.

"Time will tell."

"What do you mean, time will tell? Does that mean it's possible for me to reach Leo? I don't want Leo to be alone in the Aphotic. If I could just be with him, even if it meant me perishing in the Aphotic with him, then I'd choose it. Please, tell me more. I'd like to understand," said Aileen.

"Don't concern yourself with understanding. Time will tell you where you can and can't go."

"Okay," said Aileen.

She was content to let it go, but felt a little defeated.

"Would you like to see Leo's galaxy?" The white shadow's fair voice remained as it was when Aileen had first heard it, without rise or fall.

"We can see Leo's galaxy? Yes, please show me," said Aileen. She looked off into the sky of Portum Lux, wondering which shining speck of light could be from Leo's galaxy.

"Very well, then. I will show you Leo's galaxy. But first, you must close your eyes."

Hesitant and confused, Aileen did as she was asked.

"Okay, now open your eyes."

Aileen opened her eyes and found herself cosmically suspended. Star systems and globules dangled all around her. Pastel and neon glows alternated, filling the dark spherical canvas of her surroundings. Pulling her focus from the depths of space, she looked for her hands. She found each, but they weren't as they were. They had been transfigured into light. She quickly examined the remainder of her body and found the same thing. Even her clothes were light. She turned to find the white shadow floating beside her, no longer an intruder but a traveling companion.

"What's happened to me?" asked Aileen.

"You've changed to light."

"Does that mean I'm a Quasar?" asked Aileen.

"Not yet, you are still a Nebula."

Aileen continued to take in her new form. She didn't feel warm or cold, just a mild tingle coursing through her body. With a lean, she began to spin slowly, a smile settling on her face. As she spun, she became more aware of her surroundings, and the beauty of the stars and distant galaxies, each shining quite brightly in different hues of red, orange, and blue. One glow stood out amongst the others, not for its brightness, but for its faintness. Situated far off, the glow seemed more secluded than all the other cosmic matter in view. It sat lonely, enclosed by a small slice of black space. Aileen leaned forward and moved in the direction of the isolated glow.

As she drew closer, the glow came into focus. The black that surrounded the dim glow was smattered with distant bits of light. The dim glow revealed itself to be a galaxy. Her approach continued, with the galaxy's mass filling more and more of the dark void in front of her. Aileen's motion stopped. The galaxy loomed before her, large and expansive, though still quite far away. Its shape was that of a disc, slowly spinning clockwise from her viewpoint. Swirling bands of stars, systems, and matter branched out from the galaxy's center. Micro chaos summed to produce macro beauty, as the giant galaxy filled its residence among the cosmos.

Aileen observed the galactic behemoth, whose beauty and grandeur was matched only by its silence. From her position, the galaxy, still many light years away, was odd to behold as it seemed such a large object would be accompanied by sound. The quiet, though, seemed fitting because the mass was somehow more beautiful and majestic in silence.

Aileen reveled in the sight. She gazed all over the galaxy, singling out and appreciating what she considered to be little "poofs" of stardust. Of course, if she were next to those poofs of stardust, they would reveal themselves to be intense and devasting energy reactions on scales difficult for the mind to comprehend. No matter; from far away, she appreciated the beauty and the wondrous networks of light strung throughout the galaxy like veins. Finally, the young Celestial focused her attention on the heart of the galaxy. She recognized it. The galaxy, and its heart, belonged to Leo.

At first warm and sweet, the feeling she experienced as she stared into the heart of Leo's galaxy began to erode. She felt something else. A strange flash caught the corner of her eye, away from the galaxy's heart. Small sections of the galaxy, here and there, began to flicker. One small cluster of stars and energy went dark before recovering and regaining their light. As soon as that cluster had regained its light, another small section or vein within the galaxy would do the same. The flickering, like the surge and dissipation of power, became more prevalent, happening more frequently and in larger sections.

"What's happening to him?" Aileen said to the white shadow, who had stayed by her side.

"What you see happening to Leo's galaxy reflects what is happening to Leo. He is slowly succumbing to the effects of being held prisoner in the Aphotic. As Leo's hold on life is weakened, so, too, is his galaxy's hold on light."

"Please, tell me, is there anything that can be done to save him?" said Aileen.

"Time will tell."

"Please, tell me!" said Aileen.

"Do not concern yourself with understanding. Time will tell if Leo can or cannot be saved."

"Whatever," Aileen said, feeling defeated once again.

"Would you like to see your galaxy?" Her companion's voice remained fair, unmoved by her emotion.

"My galaxy?" said Aileen.

"Yes. You, like Leo, are a Celestial. You, like Leo and all other Celestials, have a galaxy, which is synonymous with your being."

"Woah. Yes, I would like to see it," Aileen said softly.

With that, they departed from Leo's galaxy and headed toward Aileen's. As they traveled, she remembered Sam explaining, when they first arrived on Tourlitis, that she was a Celestial and that all Celestials corresponded with a galaxy. She didn't fully grasp or appreciate the implications of Sam's words at the time. Now, while traveling at a quantum rate to see herself in galaxy form, the implications of what Sam had told her sank in fully. She was not a normal little girl, but rather a massive swirling cluster of cosmic beauty infinitely larger than Earth—the planet she had believed was her only residence, when in fact, she was also residing elsewhere in the universe, as a galaxy.

Aileen allowed the contemplation of her being to pass from her thoughts, and instead took in the sights of the universe as they passed like mountains on a Western highway. The quantum speed at which they traveled was faster than light, allowing them to cross great distances and pass many galaxies of different shapes and sizes. To Aileen, it felt similar to driving through a nice neighborhood, but instead of appreciating beautiful houses, she admired a different kind of home—galactic residencies. Each galaxy was unique in size, shape, color, and elements, like the unique genetics found in each living being. It was among these passing galaxies that something dark caught her eye.

"Wait. Stop!" said Aileen.

Her request to stop came as they moved through an intergalactic zone, a void common among the cosmos.

"Yes? What is it?"

"That there? What is that?" said Aileen.

She was looking at dark blobs suspended off in the distance. The blobs were like large black water droplets, which created a hazy interruption to the star-filled universe.

"That is dark matter."

"Why is it there?" said Aileen.

"It tore off of Dark during his banishment."

"What do you mean, it tore off?" said Aileen.

"Dark's banishment was severe, and in a term relevant to the universe, violent. As a result, Dark's exit from the universe, and into the Aphotic, had a physical impact on Dark. The transition saw pieces of Dark's flesh torn from Dark's being. These pieces of flesh still float around the universe today as dark matter, a substance that cannot be destroyed but is no longer alive apart from Dark."

"Can we go closer?" said Aileen.

"No."

"Is it dangerous?" said Aileen.

"For you it is."

"Okay. But how is it dangerous for me? What happens to a Celestial if it gets too close to dark matter?" said Aileen.

"If it got too close, a Celestial would be trapped for some time, absorbed and suspended within the dark matter. The Celestial would not perish, as the Celestial would still be in the universe and connected with its galaxy. However, the Celestial would truly be trapped, at least until someone fished the Celestial out, which could take a very long time, maybe forever."

"In that case, I agree with your caution and that we should stay away from the dark matter," said Aileen.

"Shall we continue?"

"Yes," said Aileen.

They were off again, leaving the dark matter behind. Aileen returned to inventorying galactic swirls and eddies. With time, the swirls and eddies shined brighter and more fantastic than the last. In addition, the number of swirls and eddies increased. It became necessary for their trajectory to bend and turn to avoid what was becoming a congested zone of bright and brilliant galactic matter.

Aileen's surroundings were now greater than anything she had seen before. Bright neon glows mixed with deep dark hues, as light radiated and bounced between the closely situated elements. The clusters became tighter and their speed of travel reduced until they were moving relatively slow, angling to avoid the ever-tighter masses suspended harmoniously among each other. It was odd to witness such large masses and energies balanced in such proximity without colliding.

Finally, their speed had come to a cosmic crawl. There was limited space and no darkness to be found. Brilliant light seemed to fill all voids. At last, the pair broke through the congested zone of bright matter and into a clearing.

At the center of the cosmic clearing was a beautiful spiral galaxy, in which there was no darkness. Where there would normally be darkness, as observed with other galaxies, there was a clear light filling the voids, bleeding forth from the heavily wooded jungle of interstellar matter through which they had just passed.

As Aileen turned to survey the zone through which they had come, she could see that the congested bright matter and masses formed a wall around the beautiful spiral galaxy. The wall of brilliant galactic matter looked like that of an eggshell, with the spiral galaxy at the center being the yoke. She hadn't grasped it yet, but the galaxy was hers.

They stopped short of Aileen's galaxy, a similar distance from which she had observed Leo's galaxy. The difference between the two was stark. Leo's galaxy was failing in a dark corner of the universe, while Aileen's had no darkness to be found. Only fantastic colors spread in a playful spiral.

"What is this place?" said Aileen.

"This is your home. The galaxy you're beholding is you."

"Why is it in here?" said Aileen.

She motioned to the spherical walls of cosmic matter stacked to create the enormous cosmic shield around her galaxy.

"For protection."

"Protection from what?" said Aileen.

"Not so much for protection *from* something, *but* protection to *create* something."

"And what is that?" asked Aileen.

"A new kind of light."

"What? Really? What do you mean, a new kind light?" said Aileen.

She became excited as she started to inventory all the colors and light spread across her galaxy, trying to pick out any that looked strange enough to be new.

"I'll show you."

They descended into the heart of Aileen's galaxy. Once there, she noticed what appeared to be small floating particles of light, like snow, hovering around the center of her galaxy. Looking outward from the center, the small particles of light stretched as far as she could see, each quite bright and with a white-gold hue. They offered an austere contrast against the clear light that filled the voids of her galaxy.

"Those there, the tiny flakes shining, is that it? The new kind of light?" said Aileen.

"Yes."

"It's very pretty; what is it called?" said Aileen.

"Ultralight."

"Cool. How is it different from other light?" Aileen reached out to touch a flake floating nearby.

"Ultralight has no source. Other light, as found in the universe, is generated from a source, such as a burning gas, like the star you grew up calling the sun."

"I think I understand. How does ultralight work, then?" said Aileen.

"It doesn't have to work; it just is. Think of it as pure light, perpetual."

"Okay, but where did it come from?" Aileen pressed.

Aileen wasn't allowing for time to pass between each answer and her next question.

"It's a product of your galaxy. It exists nowhere else in the universe."

"Woah, that's cool. But why doesn't it exist anywhere else?"

"It can't exist anywhere else because it's not possible for it to exist anywhere else. The purity required for the existence of ultralight is in you and your galaxy alone; it's a product of your being, of who you are. Truly, I tell you, you are unique."

"What is its purpose? Ultralight, I mean. What is the purpose of ultralight?" said Aileen.

"There, you have arrived at the correct question and the reason for you being here now, at this moment in the age of time. Let me give you a secret, which no other created being knows, regarding ultralight."

"Okay," Aileen said eagerly.

She maintained her focus on a pocket of ultralight hovering in the distance, waiting to hear the secret. However, the secret of ultralight was wordlessly given to her. In silence, she received it.

After receiving the secret of ultralight, Aileen understood why she had been brought there. With the secret in hand, she now knew she had to leave her galaxy and return to Portum Lux as soon as possible.

"Can I return to Portum Lux? I need to speak with my brother and tell him what I've learned," said Aileen.

"Yes. You may return to Portum Lux."

Aileen wasted no time. She departed on a direct route for Portum Lux, leaving her galaxy and its colossal shield behind. The time it took for her to return to Portum Lux was relatively long, considering her rate of travel was quantum and faster than light. This was a testament to the great distance between her galaxy and Portum Lux.

During the journey back, Aileen thought only of Leo, Joan, and Ko. She wondered how much time had passed, or was passing, as she barreled toward Portum Lux. Her form of travel since first leaving the Isle of Skye did not allow for the comprehension of time.

Eventually, she arrived back on Portum Lux, her feet standing once again on the firm ground of the Isle of Skye. It didn't feel like she had been gone long, but she wasn't sure. She took in the peaceful landscape and turned to speak but found she was alone. Her friend was no longer with her. She regretted not asking for her friend's name, along with many other questions, but it was of no use now. She glanced down quickly to find her body no longer glowed but had been returned to a state of flesh and bone. Aileen scanned the lush green vegetation of Skye, thinking about what she had just been party to.

She didn't know it at the moment, but she had just experienced two distinct powers reserved for Celestials. The first, was transfiguration to light. Aileen did not accomplish this on her own accord. The second, was traveling as a quantum beam. Aileen did manage this on her own, a possibility she was suspicious of as she arrived back to Portum Lux on her own. Such ability did not complete what was possible for Celestials, the extent of which, in its various forms, was of course unknown to Aileen. The young Nebula would learn of such things as she grew closer to becoming a Quasar.

Transforming into a quantum beam was not synonymous with how Arcs or Scants traveled. They each had their own means for moving around the universe. A Celestial utilizing a quantum beam involved a conversion of the Celestial's physical body into a series of particles capable of moving much faster than light. A drastic and severe transformation, it remained painless for the Celestial. While able to maintain its capacity to think, all other senses for the Celestial stayed numb when moving as a quantum beam.

Aileen knew where she had to go. She needed to find Ko and tell him the secret she had learned regarding ultralight. She thought he would know what to do next.

Aileen no longer needed the ships of Portum Lux to travel between the isles. Instead, Aileen confirmed her suspicions and transformed into a quantum beam for the second time in her young life, flashing to the Isle of Eclaireur to find her brother.

Arriving on the Isle of Eclaireur, Aileen found herself in a large valley. The valley was oval-shaped, contained a lake, and was surrounded by high mountains. Aileen stood with her back to the lake as she scanned the grounds.

In the sky above, she saw a dark flash. The flash was quickly followed by another flash. A second sequence of flashes occurred in the sky, then a third sequence of flashes. Each sequence of flashes revealed one silhouette of a body appearing and disappearing, followed by another body appearing and disappearing. The motion was too fast for Aileen to make anything out other than the brief outline of two bodies. The silhouettes blipped near, then far, and at times, way off in the distance, high on a mountain side.

Suddenly, a man appeared standing a few feet from Aileen, wearing what appeared to be a potato sack with holes cut for sleeves. The man did not disappear this time. He remained looking down at Aileen with a puzzled look strewn across his grizzled face. WHAM!

The grizzled man stumbled under the blow, moving sideways a few steps before dropping to one knee. Standing where the man had stood before, and looking down at him with a giant grin, was Ko.

"I got ya, Grubb! HA!" said Ko.

He was quite pleased to have caught Grubb with what he thought was a fair strike.

Grubb didn't respond or look at Ko as he maintained his kneeling position. Grubb's focus remained on Aileen, who was standing silently in the same spot she had been since arriving on Eclaireur. Ko realized that Grubb's focus was elsewhere, and he followed his instructor's stare to where Aileen was standing.

"Aileen! What are you doing here?" said Ko.

Ko rushed in and wrapped Aileen in a hug and she wrapped him right back. After a moment, he let go, held her at an arm's distance, and smiled. She matched his smile with an even bigger one.

"You won't believe where I've been," said Aileen.

She beamed at her brother as she began to tell him about her cosmic journey. She detailed her visit to Leo's failing galaxy, passing by the dark matter, and the experience of seeing her own galaxy. Lastly, Aileen shared the secret of ultralight, which had been revealed to her, and which she hoped they could use to save Leo from the Aphotic.

CHAPTER TEN
SORDARA

Joan entered the prison cell of Sordara. The Scant stood before her. She walked at an angle toward one side of Sordara, until she began to circle the Scant. Sordara silently turned, confined by the prison's light, keeping her eyes locked on the Arc. Joan completed three quarters of a circle around Sordara before pausing and backing up until she felt a wall. Joan held her hands behind her back as she leaned her weight against the wall. Joan appeared cool, but internally, she wrestled to maintain hope.

Joan had lost count of how many times she had entered the chamber of Sordara since arriving in Mouro. It had been almost two months now. Under the guidance of Andromeda and Sam, there had been hope that Joan could extract something real from Sordara that could lead to Leo's rescue. This hope had driven Joan to visit the prisoner exhaustively, spending most of her time on Mouro in Sordara's presence. In that time, Joan had tried everything: threats, pleas, reason, indirection, relevance, and irrelevance, with nothing to show.

Sordara had been most cruel in her dealings with Joan. She went further than just not revealing secrets; she hadn't spoken at all. In Joan's countless hours and days beseeching Sordara, the Light Reaper hadn't offered words or expression. She instead stared at Joan unceasingly, not in a manner that acknowledged Joan but in a way that made Joan feel as if Sordara was looking through her.

Sordara's cruel tactic had an exacting effect on Joan. Though Joan, having spent a great deal of time in Sordara's presence, hadn't visibly broken down, her heart and mind were terrorized by the Light Reaper. She could feel Leo's time nearing its end; he had been in the Aphotic too long. She had been on Portum Lux, and in Mouro, for too long. She was failing her brother.

Joan entered Sordara's cell this time, like many times before, after strategizing on tactics with Andromeda and Sam. Andromeda and Sam had remained supportive and optimistic, though they, like Joan, had been losing hope in Sordara proving useful. Prior to Joan entering Sordara's cell this time, the three of them had agreed to a dangerous stunt to draw Sordara out of her silence. The stunt was Sam's idea, which Andromeda vehemently objected to at first. After much debate and conjecture, the contrarian within Sam won out, and Andromeda had acquiesced to allowing Sam's idea to go forward.

It was this idea with which Joan was armed as she stood in Sordara's midst once more. Sordara remained transfixed on Joan. The Arc tried her best to match Sordara's glare, to look through her. Physically, there was not much to look through. Sordara's frame was skeletal. She was gaunt and appeared malnourished, her head draped by ratty blonde hair framing sunken black eyes.

Sordara's body appeared jagged through the black fabric covering her body. The fabric fell to the floor, covering her feet.

Sordara's posture was braced but relaxed under currents of light that wrapped her legs, arms, and torso, restraining her from any movement toward Joan.

Sordara did not blink. Neither did Joan as she took a deep breath.

"I'm out of time, but you know that. For all I know, it's too late, and the Aphotic has taken Leo from me forever. It should be clear to you by now what my desires are. Not only what I want, but why I want it. It's also clear to me what you want, but what's not clear is why you want it. I've thought a lot about it, about you, Sordara, trying to understand why you want the things you want. Why do you serve Dark? What has Dark done to you, that you'd find joy in the destruction of life?" said Joan.

Sordara remained unmoved by Joan's intro. Joan allowed a few silent seconds to pass before continuing.

"Of course, I don't expect you to tell me 'the why' behind what you do. For all I know, you might not even know why you do what you do. Perhaps you've been compromised—your heart, mind, and being—to the point there's nothing alive behind the wheel of your actions. Absent fully understanding your complexities, Sordara, I must focus on your simplest actions. Actions that don't require your explanation for me to understand. When you, or any Scant, takes a being to the Aphotic, I know you feel something, some sort of joy. It'd be natural for you to attach your joy to something, to value something as the provider of that joy. Maybe you've attached your joy to an article or object, maybe a fabric?" said Joan.

Sordara's eyes flashed briefly in response to Joan's last question. Joan shifted her weight off the wall of the cell, freeing her hands to fall by her side. She walked toward Sordara and stopped within arm's reach of the prisoner. Joan silently waved a hand through the streaming light constraining Sordara. Joan leaned into the Light Reaper, her face nearly touching Sordara's.

"I want to give you something you want," whispered Joan.

Sordara's arcane stare faltered. She was now looking at Joan, no longer looking through her, in anticipation. Sordara's body tightened against her restraints.

Joan leaned away from Sordara, and with a wave of her hand, motioned for Sordara's restraints to be removed. The light in the cell obeyed and retreated from Sordara's body, leaving Sordara unrestrained and within arm's distance of Joan. Sordara gaped around the cell, weary of a trick but at the same time enjoying what was an unimaginable development. Coming to terms with her freedom, Sordara turned her focus back to her foe. Joan reached out and grabbed Sordara, and through a flash, warped Sordara to the Great Chamber of Mouro.

Sordara shielded her eyes against the white light of the Chamber, it's view slowly coming into focus. The Light Reaper found herself among the Veils of Mouro's imprisoned Scants. The Veils numbered by the thousands in the great room, each taut and stretched in place by the light of the chamber.

Her eyes darted from Veil to Veil. Sordara cringed for the tortured Veils. She wanted to set them free. That thought, setting the Veils free, consumed Sordara as her mind raced with possibilities. What if she, Sordara, were responsible for freeing all the captured Veils, and in turn Scants, from Mouro? Dark would be beyond pleased with her. Dark would hold her in higher esteem than any creature in the universe, above all other Light Reapers. Dark would have to consider her his bride; there'd be no other endearment, besides bride, appropriate to reciprocate the gift of her giving Dark all the captives of Mouro.

Sordara's thought was interrupted by the sight of her own Veil. No longer daydreaming of her glory with Dark, the silent Light Reaper allowed a short gasp followed by a smile as she moved toward her Veil. Sordara prepared to touch her Veil, to free it, and bend it to her desires once again. The prospect caused Sordara to salivate. Her body relaxed, and she felt at peace for the first time since her capture, the longing for her precious Veil nearing its end.

Sordara broke her silence, speaking to her Veil as she approached it.

"I see you, my dearest … " said Sordara.

But Sordara, sensing something else, cut her address short. She began to feel a new sensation. One of panic.

Joan had stayed close to Sordara, waiting for the right moment. The something Sordara sensed was Joan's hand moving toward her shoulder. Sordara realized the trap. She lunged, trying to escape, trying to reach her Veil, her dearest. It was too late. Sordara's Veil and the chamber disappeared from her view. Sordara felt the warp Joan pulled her through, then the familiar burn of light glowing once again around her restrained body. Like a dream, her Veil had vanished.

Sordara was back in her cell, bound in the chains of light, and face to face with the young Arc who had completed the cruel trick of warping Sordara to, and away from, her heart's greatest desire. Joan had allowed Sordara to feel as if her Veil were hers again.

Minutes passed as Joan and Sordara locked eyes, each enraged and filled with hate toward the other. Sordara cracked, filling the volume of her cell with a loud cackling laugh. Sordara's raspy voice followed.

"How clever! The little mouse has a mean streak! Well, here I am, little mouse. I'll tell you; just ask and I'll tell you. You won't like it, little mouse, you won't like it at all. You'll see, my silence is better, much better than anything I'll tell you. Ask away, please hurry and ask; I can't wait any longer!" said Sordara.

"My brother, Leo, he—" started Joan, but she was cut off by Sordara.

"There! Yes, now we're there. Your brother, Leo, the Celestial of what must be the most pitiful galaxy, worth hardly any lumens. That said, even the most pitiful of galaxies must go, must be put out, to make way for Dark. I know what you're thinking, little mouse, but it doesn't matter! Your brother is gone; he belongs to the Aphotic!" said Sordara.

Joan ignored Sordara's outbursts and tried again, fighting back the fear that Sordara could be telling the truth.

"My brother, Leo, he was taken by a tall and slender Scant, a man with white hair, a white-blond beard and mustache, sunken eyes, and dressed in black. He was quite gaunt and quite tall. His beard was short and followed the line of his jaw. Do you know this Scant?" said Joan.

"How foolish, little mouse. Your profile sounds like all Scants. I can't say if I know the Scant. It's unlikely, you see, as I don't socialize much with the others. We don't have much in common, you see. I'm a Light Reaper; other Scants don't see the dark like I do," said Sordara.

Sordara appeared to nearly burst with pride as she reflected on her status above other Scants.

"This one, the Scant who took my brother, he twitched. That's right, his body twitched, and his face jerked when he was excited. Or maybe it's when he's angry, but either way, his body seemed to convulse. He also had red eyes. Do many Scants have red eyes? You don't seem to," said Joan.

Joan looked closely at Sordara's eyes, searching the dark spheres for a hint of red. Sordara released another cackle.

"Ha-hee-hee, yes, it turns out I do know the Scant of which you speak. That's not good, of course, for you, that I know him. The red eyes are unique, but not enough to give him away. The twitch, that twitch, is what gives him away. Yes, he's a twitchy one. The best news is that, are you ready? The best news is that he's a Light Reaper, like me. How delightful! I'm not sure if you can grasp it, little mouse. I'm sure you can't, so I'll help you. Light Reapers can go where other Scants can't! To be a Light Reaper is to be intimately known by Dark! How delightful it is that I know the one who took your brother. What a dark creature, who took your brother. Yes, take it from me, there are few darker than Atros."

"Atros?" said Joan.

"Yes, Atros the Light Reaper took your brother. Ha-hee-hee. Your brother's doom is guaranteed. I imagine, yes, I imagine that your brother is in a corner of the Aphotic that even I can't find. Atros is quite—yes, very much—famous for residing in, how should I say it, the darkest and most sordid layers of the Aphotic. Places where dark takes on never known shades of nothingness."

Every time Sordara spoke, it struck Joan like a blow. Joan, however, gritted her teeth and kept her focus, forcing Sordara's words to glance by her. If Joan showed weakness, or sadness, then Sordara would have won, with Joan having to retreat from the conversation and leaving Sordara content to settle back into her silence.

"I plan to find Atros," said Joan.

"Little mouse, I'm quite pleased to tell you it's impossible. You'll never find Atros. He's a Light Reaper. Light Reapers are not found, you see. We do the finding," said Sordara.

"You were found, Sordara, weren't you? I mean, you're here with me, right? A prisoner on the Isle of Mouro. Light Reapers must not always do the finding; they must be found sometimes, or you wouldn't be here on Portum Lux," said Joan.

Sordara snarled, "You know nothing, little mouse."

Joan's observation, of Sordara being a Light Reaper who had been caught, caused Sordara to retreat slightly. Joan could see she had caused Sordara to slip into thought. Sordara suddenly seemed removed from the room, no longer focused on Joan. The vinegar of Sordara's outbursts was subdued. Joan sought to bring Sordara's focus back, without inciting the Light Reaper.

"I know some things, but there's still much I don't understand. Can you tell me why you serve Dark? Why love Dark when you could be embraced by Light?" said Joan.

"Little mouse, if only you could know. One day you will know. Yes. When Light is extinguished and there is only Dark, all will know and embrace Dark. You see, Light wants to control you, to own you, to limit you, when you could be so much more. The true chains of creation are the chains of Light. I once was like you, yes, little mouse, like you, crushed under the rule of Light. I didn't know it at the time. I didn't know I was bound and chained, until Dark touched me and opened my eyes. Dark freed me, removing my dependence on Light and aiding me in becoming something more. Under Light, I was a created being, but with Dark, I am begotten, independent of Light and my own master. Yes, my own master. Yes, my own. Sordara is her own."

Sordara's raspy voice trailed off, pleased with the assertion of being her own.

"You are not your own," said Joan.

"Yes, little mouse, I am," said Sordara.

"You are a slave," said Joan.

"I am no slave, no, I am not. I am the administer of my being, of the time around me. Yes, little mouse, I initiate my desires. There is nothing imposed on me that I don't first sign off on. Dark sees to it. Yes, Dark keeps me free," said Sordara.

"You are a slave to your Veil. I've seen it. Your Veil controls you. Who controls your Veil, Sordara?" said Joan.

"I do!" snapped Sordara.

"No, you don't. Dark does. Dark controls your Veil, and in turn, Dark controls you," said Joan.

"Enough! Little mouse, little rat! Yes, you're not a mouse. You're a rat! Arc filth, chained and blinded by your precious Light," said Sordara.

"Tell me, how are you your own, Sordara? Please, test yourself. You long for your Veil, you long to please Dark. Dark has you. You are not your own. You've been sold a freedom laced with dependence. How are you your own?"

Sordara's rage was kindled. Joan could see it racing through the Light Reaper's body.

"Yes, I long to please Dark, only for the freedom that Dark has granted me. It is an exchange, the give and take of the relationship I have with Dark. With Light, there is no exchange, no give and take, only Light taking. Yes, I long for my Veil. But hear me, hear me when I say, little mouse, that my Veil is truly mine. It is mine in ways you can't comprehend, little mouse. I need you to pay attention to what I'm saying."

Sordara paused until she was sure she had Joan's full attention. Joan remained silent. Satisfied, Sordara continued.

"My Veil and I have taken little ones before. Very many. Yes, very many. Nebula Celestials like your sweet brother, Leo. I'm angry with myself for not keeping count of how many Celestials have gone black under my Veil. Sometimes I just want to scream, 'How many!' To not know is infuriating. Is it a hundred? Is it five hundred? Is it a thousand? It never occurred to me to count. It's no matter. The number does not change me. All I want is to take, you see, to watch the light of little ones be squeezed under the fabric of my bidding. That's what my Veil is, the fabric of my bidding. It's a small thing for me to extinguish Celestials, like your brother, and their galaxies. A small gift for me to give Dark, in return for the freedom Dark has given me. Each time they fade, writhing against the Aphotic, it leaves a little more room for Dark, and in turn, a little more room for me."

Sordara paused again. Joan remained silent.

"Little mouse, what I'm trying to say is that my Veil is mine, and I am mine, as we are the only ones who together have watched a thousand little Celestials, just like your brother, disappear forever in the Aphotic. A thousand wonderful moments that only we know. I am mine, I am my Veil's, and we are each other."

Sordara finished smugly, happy she had shared her grim history with Joan in a way that she believed would eradicate any remaining hope in Joan.

Joan knew Sordara was telling the truth. Sordara had indeed seen to the death of a thousand Nebula Celestials, maybe more. Joan could see Sordara was a strange kind of insane, embodying an unnatural existence bent on anti-hope. Being around a silent Sordara had been draining on Joan, but the short amount of time conversing with Sordara was taking a different toll on Joan, a life-sucking toll. Sordara exhibited an incapacity for anything but taking joy in death. Thoughts of Leo, and small pangs of hope, kept Joan from giving up.

"I'm sorry for you," said Joan.

Sordara was caught off guard. She did not expect pity from the Arc.

"I'm sorry that you've lost your dearest. I know how you feel," said Joan.

"What are you playing at, little mouse?" said Sordara.

"Your Veil. You've lost it, forever. You can never return to Dark, to the one who freed you. Your Veil is an eternal prisoner, and as such, your passage to the Aphotic has been taken away. Even if you were able to escape from Mouro, your Veil would remain in the chamber. You'd have no way of returning to the Aphotic. It must be sad, knowing you'll never draw close to Dark again," said Joan.

Sordara's face narrowed. "Don't play with me, little mouse. What game are you playing? Yes, it's a game! You don't feel anything for me, just as I don't feel anything for you."

"I'm not like you. I can feel for others. I've lost something. I've lost Leo. You've lost something. You've lost your Veil, your dearest. It's okay; with time in Mouro, surrounded by light, I'm sure you'll learn to feel, to acknowledge your loss, to mourn, and maybe eventually to be reformed," said Joan.

"Stop. You're playing something," said Sordara.

"No, I'm not playing at anything." Joan's voice raised in frustration at Sordara's inability to recognize compassion. "It's sad. Do you not see it, Scant?" said Joan.

"See what, little mouse?" said Sordara.

"That you and I are the same! We are both empty, both lost, both forever without that which we love most!" said Joan.

Sordara allowed a pause before releasing yet another cackle in the face of the broken Arc.

"Ha-hee-hee! Little mouse! Yes, that's what you are. You know nothing! Mice know more! You can keep my Veil. Mouro can keep my dearest. But Mouro can't keep me from the Aphotic. Mouro won't keep me at all. There's another way, you see, another way to reach the Aphotic, to be with Dark. A passage only Light Reapers know. So, you're wrong, little mouse! You have lost your love, but I have not lost mine. I will leave this place, will find my way back to the Aphotic, and will begin with a new cut of fabric, a new piece of Dark, a new Veil! In time, I will know my dearest again. A black hole is all that I need to reach the Aphotic!"

That's it, Joan thought. A black hole. A secret about the Aphotic. Her efforts, along with Sam's and Andromeda's, had worked.

Joan quickly digested the concept that black holes provided another way to the Aphotic separate from the Veil of a Scant. With this secret in hand, Joan made up her mind immediately. She didn't know how yet, but a black hole would be her way to the Aphotic and to Leo. For Joan, warping through a black hole to save her brother and perishing was a better alternative to doing nothing.

Sordara had watched Joan closely, but the young Arc offered no reaction to Sordara's triumphant proclamation. She could see Joan was pondering, contemplating, and no longer paying attention to Sordara. Then, Sordara realized what she had done. She had said too much, revealing the secret of black holes and restoring a sense of hope to the young Arc. Sordara sought to belittle the error.

"Ha-hee-hee, I know what you're thinking, Arc. It can't be done. Only a Light Reaper can pass through a black hole. Even if you could find a way through, you'd never find your brother. The Aphotic is an immeasurable expanse, and you won't know where to look. That's right, you won't know where to look. Like I said before, Atros is known for burying Celestials in the most remote zones of the Aphotic, places where no other has gone before. Even I couldn't find Atros, or your brother, if I tried. So how would a little mouse like you manage to find him, assuming you could even find a way to pass through a black hole and reach the Aphotic?" She was satisfied she had once again extinguished Joan's hope.

"That'll be all, Sordara. Thank you for the information. Sam and Andromeda, thank you as well," said Joan.

She warped out of the cell, leaving Sordara alone, left to brood about having been bested by the young Arc, tricked from her silence and into sharing too much.

Joan found Andromeda waiting outside. Andromeda, who had monitored the entirety of Joan and Sordara's meeting, wore a sly smile as if to say they had gotten away with something.

Joan beamed. She wasn't sure why. She knew she couldn't travel to a black hole, as there would be no oxygen or atmosphere to keep her body from imploding. Even if she could survive passing through a black hole, she knew nothing about the Aphotic. For all she knew, upon entering the Aphotic, she would be crushed by an incomprehensible state of existence. And even if she wasn't crushed, how would she locate Leo in the Aphotic? She believed it when Sordara said the Aphotic was an immeasurable expanse. How could she find Leo in such an expanse? Finally, if she did somehow find Leo, how would she rescue and bring him back from the Aphotic? What if they came across Atros?

The challenges of Leo's rescue compounded to make for long odds. Joan recognized this, but she still beamed nonetheless as she greeted Andromeda. She felt she had discovered something significant in Sordara revealing the secret of black holes. Something that could lead to saving her brother from a blackness worse than death.

"Well, what do you think?" said Joan, grinning up at Andromeda.

"I think the secrets of Dark are many, and that you have found an important one. Black holes have long been known as tears in the universe, which resulted from the banishment of Dark by Light, though we've never paid them much attention, mostly steering clear due to their dangerous nature. The thought of a Scant using anything but its Veil to travel to the Aphotic never crossed my mind. Learning that Light Reapers use black holes as back doors to the Aphotic is a valuable discovery. Something we may be able to exploit in the battle with Dark," said Andromeda.

"Yes! I knew it," said Joan, her hope rising with Andromeda's validation of the discovery.

"What next? What do we do? What do I do? Can you, or someone else, take me to a black hole? Is there something that can be done so I can survive a black hole?" said Joan.

Joan spoke fast to Andromeda, anxious to save her brother, or die trying. Before Andromeda could answer, Joan tacked on one last question as she noticed a missing presence.

"Where is Sam?"

"Sam returned to Tourlitis. His attention is required elsewhere for the time being. As for you, you need to travel to the Isle of Eclaireur and find those you traveled to Portum Lux with," said Andromeda.

"Ko and Aileen?" said Joan.

"Yes," said Andromeda.

"Why? What about black holes? Didn't you hear what I said? I must find a way to Leo. I don't have time to go anywhere that doesn't lead me closer to him," said Joan.

"I understand. I have it on good authority that it is with your friends on Eclaireur where you might find what you are seeking. If there is a way for you to travel through a black hole, and reach your brother in the Aphotic, it is on the Isle of Eclaireur where you will find it," said Andromeda.

"Okay. Then I will go there. If I never see you again, thank you for helping me," said Joan.

"It is I who should be thanking you for what you did with Sordara. Know that, as you go forth, you have an ally in Mouro," said Andromeda.

"That's good to know. Thank you," said Joan.

Joan followed Andromeda's instruction. She left Mouro for Eclaireur, to seek out her friends and maybe, she hoped, even a black hole.

CHAPTER ELEVEN
GRUBB

Joan arrived at the lighthouse of Eclaireur. Grubb was there waiting for her. Both showed looks of impatience, the kind that comes from being given an instruction without a timeline. Their looks revealed to one another that each had been directed by a Celestial. After quick introductions, they warped into the mountains of Eclaireur.

Arriving in a clearing, Joan stood facing the base of a tall mountain centered in an enclave of lesser peaks. Like Ko before her, Joan listened as Grubb explained where she was and how the mountain was known as the Alveare of Eclaireur, the great home to Arcs across the universe. Captivated, she felt a connection with the mountain, as if she had known the Alveare her entire life. Joan felt at home.

She turned to survey the great courtyard, which flowed from the base of the Alveare. She admired the surrounding peaks and their beauty. Lowering her eyes, the lake of Eclaireur came into view and far away, she immediately recognized the Veil of the lake.

Joan froze. The Veils of Mouro had been frightening, even in chains. A Veil out in the open, free from chains, sparked a terror in her.

"We need to leave, immediately," said Joan.

"No, lass, we don't. We're in no danger from that Veil. It's just lookin' after somethin' in the lake that once belonged to its Scant. There'll be time fer ye to meet that Veil an' see that it's harmless later. In the meantime, I believe there's two in the mountain that ye're eager to see," said Grubb.

Grubb's calm demeanor regarding the Veil of the lake made Joan comfortable enough to let her guard down. She turned from the lake and gave her attention to the Alveare.

"Yes, are they in there?" She motioned to the great mountain.

"They are," said Grubb.

"And do you know why I'm here?"

"I do. Me sorrow fer ye is bigger than these mountains. It hurts to think o' ye brother in the Aphotic. It hurts to think o' ye, bein' so young an' havin' to face such darkness. I don't intend to make ye feel better, or to have pity on ye. I just want ye to know that I understan'," said Grubb.

"Thanks," said Joan.

Grubb nodded before shrugging the emotion off.

"Befer we enter, do ye' mind if I ask ye' where ye' were befer comin' here? Based on the two I got in there right now, an' now ye arrivin', it doesn't feel like the type o' visit I'm used to. The Celestial that's here, the young one, has been sayin' some crazy things. And her Arc, Ko, who I think ye know, has an aptitude fer bendin' that most don't. I'm curious if ye're as strange as them two?" said Grubb.

"I was in Mouro visiting a Scant who goes by Sordara. Have you heard of her?" said Joan.

"Sordara is in Mouro! Ye could o' told me anythin' else, truly anythin', an' it wouldn't be as difficult to believe as ye tellin' me that Sordara, the Light Reaper, has been taken prisoner in Mouro. How I'd like to see that," said Grubb, with a look of wonder.

"It's true. Andromeda has her," said Joan.

"Well, that does it. The three o' ye are quare strange. Let's get ye to the other two," said Grubb.

Grubb and Joan warped into the Alveare. Once inside, Joan followed Grubb through the tunnels of the mountain as they searched for Ko and Aileen. They checked, but Ko and Aileen weren't in the Green Cavern, the galley, or the great mess hall with all the empty tables. Grubb looked in observatories high in the mountain, and even the mines deep underground, but without any sign of Ko and Aileen. The last vast and unchecked voids of the mountain contained the libraries of Eclaireur. That is where Grubb and Joan went next.

Grubb and Joan made their way down a long tunnel angling toward the heart of the mountain. The tunnel offered many doors to smaller caverns filled with books and manuscripts. Passing the smaller rooms and following the tunnel to its completion, at the heart of the mountain, brought Grubb and Joan to the greatest treasure of Eclaireur, the Library of Arcs. There were no doors separating the end of the tunnel from the heart of the mountain. Grubb and Joan simply exited the mouth of the tunnel and were greeted by a towering void rising almost as far as the eye could see. The empty space they had entered seemed like a mountain within the mountain.

Beneath the towering void was a vast floor filled with books and papers stacked so high one had to strain one's neck to glimpse the tops. Grubb and Joan began to walk among the towering stacks of books in search of Ko and Aileen. The smell of molding paper and untouched dust coated the air. After clearing a few rows, Grubb and Joan rounded a corner to find what they were looking for: Ko and Aileen, sitting on the floor flanked by a spread of open books and loose papers.

"Joan! You're here!" said Aileen.

Aileen jumped up and ran to Joan, giving her a hug.

"Hello, pretty girl," said Joan as she embraced Aileen.

"You won't believe where I've been," said Aileen.

"Try me; I think I'd believe anything now," said Joan.

"I went to Leo's galaxy, then my own, and I came back with something that might be able to help Leo!" said Aileen.

"Wait, you went to Leo's galaxy? How?" said Joan.

"Let's save that story for later, Aileen. It's good to see you, Joan," said Ko, as he stood and walked toward Joan and Aileen.

"It's good to see you too," said Joan.

The three friends stood amongst the pile of books Ko and Aileen had gathered. Grubb stepped away, allowing the friends time to catch up.

"Do either of you know how long we've been on Portum Lux? It's hard to tell, and I'm afraid my brother is out of time," said Joan.

"When I visited his galaxy, it was still there, but it was losing light," said Aileen.

"Sam said your brother could last the equivalent of two months, give or take, in the Aphotic. Days aren't the same on Portum Lux as they are on Earth, but time is time, and it certainly feels as if we've been here longer than two months. We must assume that your brother is out of time, with the Aphotic being near to finishing him at any moment, during any hour. We must move fast. Aileen has something we hope can help your brother," said Ko.

"Is that something the reason you're in here with all of these books?" said Joan.

"Yes. Apparently, Aileen has not stayed on Portum Lux during our time here. She traveled somewhere I still don't fully understand. But as I said, we can discuss that when we have more time. Regardless of where Aileen has been, she has something she thinks can help Leo. What do you call it, Aileen?" said Ko.

"It's ultralight." Aileen held up a small black bag, signaling its contents. "I sort of know how it works, and I think I can use it to reach the Aphotic. But that's not the big issue. The problem is we don't know where the Aphotic is."

"How can light be kept in a bag?" said Joan, eager to see Aileen's discovery.

"It's strange, but ultralight is different from normal light. Normal light, like the shine from a star, is the result of burning gas. The burning gas is the source of the light. Once the gas burns up, the shining star will stop. Ultralight doesn't depend on a gas, or anything else. It will shine forever," said Aileen.

Aileen opened the bag and released the ultralight she had brought back from her galaxy. Though the bag was small, the ultralight poured out in the thousands, filling the heart of the mountain. Joan and Ko gaped at the brilliant tiny glows floating around them. Joan reached out to touch one, but her finger passed through it. She didn't feel anything.

"They're not hard, or soft, or hot, or cold. They're just light. The only other thing I know about them is they do what I want them to," said Aileen.

In response to Aileen, the ultralight, which had spread throughout the hull of the mountain, returned to Aileen. It instantly funneled back into her little black bag. The brilliant light had disappeared from the heart of the mountain just as quickly as it had filled it.

"Amazing," said Joan. "How did you do that? You didn't say anything."

"In my head I say what I want it to do, and the ultralight listens," said Aileen.

"I see, and how does it all fit in that tiny bag, after filling all of this?" said Joan, motioning a hand toward the large void above them.

"Normal light doesn't require volume or take up space. Aileen's light, I mean, ultralight must be similar," said Ko.

"That makes sense. It's quite brilliant, Aileen. You've amazed me, but how could it help my brother?" said Joan.

"I think the ultralight can take us to the Aphotic," said Aileen.

"How's that?" said Joan.

"I'm still figuring it out, but I know it will work. I think that's why I have it, to reach the Aphotic, to save Leo," said Aileen.

"Then what are we waiting for? Let's go," said Joan.

"Well, like Aileen mentioned before, we don't know where the Aphotic is. The ultralight may work, but only if Aileen knows where to aim it. That's why we're in the library. We were hoping to find a manuscript, or something, which might tell us where the Aphotic is. Really, Portum Lux would do well by adopting the internet, it would make our search so much easier," said Ko.

"Have you found anything useful?" asked Joan.

"No. As it stands, the only access to the Aphotic we're aware of is through the Veil of a Scant. The Aphotic doesn't exactly have coordinates," said Ko.

Joan had almost forgotten about her trip to Mouro and the reason for seeking out Ko and Aileen. Andromeda's request for her to travel to Eclaireur now made sense.

"I think it's my turn to share what I've found," said Joan. "Light Reapers can use black holes to travel back and forth from the Aphotic."

The three of them were not aware that Grubb had positioned himself inconspicuously near, around a corner of books, so he could monitor their discussion.

"What? Black holes—you mean the scary dark whirlpools where matter is crushed into an unfathomable singularity?" said Ko.

"Yes. Those black holes," said Joan.

"How did you learn this?" said Ko.

"An imprisoned Light Reaper told me," said Joan.

"You met a Light Reaper? There's a Light Reaper on Portum Lux?" said Ko.

"Yes, supposedly, she's the first Light Reaper to be captured alive and brought to Mouro. She, along with thousands of other Scants, are imprisoned by chains of light, which are controlled by a Quasar Celestial named Andromeda," said Joan.

"She? The Light Reaper you met was a female?" said Ko.

"Yes, and she's quite something. Her name is Sordara. I tried during my entire time on Mouro to get her to speak to me, to see if she would reveal any secrets of the Aphotic that could help us save Leo. She was silent like a monk, refusing to talk, no matter what I said or tried to do. It was her way of torturing me, and it was torture. Finally, Sam had the idea to let her free for a little bit, to get her to talk. It worked, and at last she spoke with me. She slipped up and revealed that Light Reapers use black holes to reach the Aphotic," said Joan.

"Sam's idea was to let a Light Reaper free around you? That seems foolish," said Ko.

"It was a little risky, but it worked. Letting Sordara taste freedom for a moment, and then shackling her again, jolted her from the silence she had been torturing me with. There's one other thing I learned from Sordara that I need to tell you," said Joan.

"What's that?" said Ko.

"Sordara told me the name of the Scant who took Leo, and your parents," said Joan.

※ ※ ※

"Oh," said Ko.

Ko was caught off guard. He realized that since arriving on Portum Lux, he had hardly thought of his parents and their fate.

"What's the Scant's name?" said Ko.

"Atros. He's a Light Reaper, like Sordara," said Joan.

"Well. That's not good, is it?" said Ko.

"No, it's not," said Joan.

Ko remained silent for a few seconds as he reflected on his parents. His mind settled into a daydream of the moments in Stono with the Scant, whom he now knew to be Atros the Light Reaper. Putting a name to the one responsible for taking his parents caused him to realize he desired revenge. He didn't want to focus on the hope of seeing his parents again; it seemed easier to imagine his revenge against Atros, making the Light Reaper pay for what he had done. Ko relished the prospect of avenging his parents, but he couldn't stay in his daydream long. In order to find Atros, he first needed to find the Aphotic.

"I'm glad we know his name. I look forward to us finding him. Hang here for a second; I'll be right back," said Ko.

Ko disappeared into a warp, leaving Joan and Aileen standing alone among the pile of books and papers.

☀ ☀ ☀

"Ko can warp?" said Joan with a surprised expression toward Aileen.

"Yep. I wish he hadn't; I wanted to tell you guys something. I'll wait until he gets back," said Aileen.

"It's amazing that Ko can warp. I don't know why I'm surprised," said Joan.

Joan hadn't realized it, but when she left Ko and Aileen two months before, she had viewed them as helpless, which to a great degree they had been. They didn't seem helpless to Joan any longer, with Ko warping around and Aileen holding a bag of something called ultralight. She thought of Aileen lying in the meadow after Stono, and she remembered how fragile the little girl had seemed.

"Aileen, how have you been since we last saw each other? Are you okay? I know it's hard to think of Stono, and to hear us talk about that Scant," said Joan.

"I'm okay. Thank you for asking. Sometimes I think about my parents and I'm sad. Mostly, though, I'm okay. I'm happy to have met you, and happy to have Ko. And it's okay if you talk about Atros. He isn't to blame," said Aileen.

"What do you mean, Atros isn't to blame?" said Joan.

"He can't help what he does. He's just a shark, doing what sharks do," said Aileen.

Before Joan could respond, Ko reappeared, his arms full of more books. Joan let her conversation with Aileen go and turned her attention back to Ko.

"How do you like warping?" said Joan.

"It's fantastic! I like it very much," said Ko.

The books in his arms shifted, causing him to shift as well.

"Can you create an obscure?" said Joan.

"I can," said Ko.

"Can you create a good one?" said Joan.

She expected to find a limit to Ko's development. Before Ko could respond, Grubb answered on his behalf.

"He can. Lad's quare good at obscurin'," said Grubb.

Grubb spoke while walking from behind a shelf of books, as if just returning from far off. His tone was naïve, suggesting he hadn't heard their discussion regarding ultralight, black holes, and Atros.

"Say, Ko, what are those books ye got there?" said Grubb.

"I found a few books on black holes, to see if they could give us clues on how to travel through one without disintegrating," said Ko.

"Ko," said Aileen, "I was going to say, before you warped away so rudely, that we don't need more books. Joan telling us about black holes is the key. You and I were trying to find out where the Aphotic is. We still don't know exactly where the Aphotic is, but we know where black holes are. Joan's given me something to aim at. That's all we need, and I can take care of the rest."

"What do you mean, you can take care of the rest?" said Ko.

He set aside the books he had gathered and focused on his sister.

"Well, when I left Portum Lux and traveled among the galaxies, I became light. I could go anywhere, except to the Aphotic. That's because the source of my light would be cut off in the Aphotic, blocking my ability to travel. However, I think I can use ultralight to provide protection while passing through a black hole. That's not the best part though. The best part is that, once through the black hole, the ultralight will continue to shine. It is its own source. There's nothing for the Aphotic to cut the ultralight off from," said Aileen.

"You can become light?" said Joan.

"It's a sign she's turnin' into a Quasar, bein' able to turn into light like that. Won't be long befer our little one here is no longer a Nebula," said Grubb.

"That's good, right? How will we know when she's reached Quasar level?" said Ko.

"Well, in addition to the quantum travelin' she's been doin', she'll be controllin' light. When great streams o' light start goin' where Aileen tells 'em, that'll signal she's a Quasar," said Grubb.

"Like how Andromeda controls light at Mouro?" said Joan.

"Somethin' like that. Though, it will take some time befer she can do with light what Andromeda can do. The important thing is, when she's fully a Quasar, she'll be out o' the reach o' Scants, untouchable by the Aphotic," said Grubb.

"Aileen, can you send me to the Aphotic with ultralight?" said Joan.

"I'm going too," said Ko.

"No, Ko," said Joan, "I can't ask you to do that. You and Aileen have done enough. If Leo perishes in the Aphotic, and I die trying to save him, it will be as it should. But if you come along and die as well, it will be unbearable for me at the end, knowing that you've been taken from Aileen."

"Neither of you can go," said Aileen.

Joan and Ko turned their attention back to Aileen.

"What do you mean?" said Joan.

"The ultralight can provide protection for passage through a black hole, but it will only work for a Celestial in the form of light. It won't be like the tunnel of light that brought us here to Portum Lux, where our bodies were protected. If I tried to take you with me in a beam of ultralight, your bodies would be exposed to space. You wouldn't make it past the sky of Portum Lux before dying," said Aileen.

Grubb had heard enough.

"Alright, that's enough o' that talk. No one is ridin' a beam o' anythin' to the Aphotic. Not ye, Ko. Not ye, Joan, an' especially not ye, Aileen. I'm sorry I let ye go on like this, but I didn't think ye'd get to the point where ye we're gonna try an' actually go the Aphotic. That's insane, an' Light itself wouldn't want me allowin' any of ye to go; it's too dangerous." said Grubb.

The image of Grubb flickered. He now held a black iron chest coated in raised symbols and strange markings. Aileen reached for her waist. The ultralight was gone. Joan and Ko heard Aileen's gasp and realized the little bag of ultralight was no longer by her side. Without detection, Grubb had warped, grabbed the bag of ultralight from Aileen, grabbed the chest he now held, and locked the bag of ultralight within the chest.

"I'm sorry, ye three, but I can't let ye do anythin' crazy. When it's done, I'll give it back, I promise," said Grubb.

Joan knew what Grubb was saying. He planned to give the ultralight back only after the Aphotic had finished Leo. That way, they'd have no reason for the risky rescue attempt. Joan's fists clenched as she began to scream at Grubb.

"When it's done! You mean, when Leo's gone! You want to wait until the Aphotic has put him out!"

"I'm sorry, lass, I truly am. I know what ye' feelin', but ye're brother is gone. No one's ever come back from the Aphotic. We can't save him, an' I can't let another Celestial go into the Aphotic after him. With certainty, if Aileen made it to the Aphotic, she wouldn't come back. Light can't lose two Celestials like that; it'd be senseless."

"Aileen! Take it back from him!" said Joan.

A few seconds passed as Aileen tried to call the ultralight to her.

"Nothing's happening. The ultralight can't feel me; it's not responding," said Aileen.

"It can't hear ye, I'm sorry. Ye're a special one, I can tell." Grubb was looking at Aileen. "I'm not sure what this ultralight is, but it's special, I know it. I don't know if ye can reach the Aphotic with it, through a black hole an' all, but I can't let ye try it. I promise, I'll give it back soon. We just need to wait."

"Don't say it like that! Say what it is! You want to wait for my brother to die," said Joan.

Joan tried to take a step toward Grubb but was held back by Ko, who sought to console her. Joan caught her breath. Ko let go of her and took a step toward Grubb himself.

"What is that?" said Ko, referring to the black iron chest in Grubb's arms.

"It's called a Rib Cage. It was made by Scants fer a heinous purpose, one we need not discuss. It serves to sever connections with light, like a small version o' the Aphotic. In this case, it's servin' to keep Aileen from accessin' the ultralight," said Grubb.

"Why would you have one of those?" said Ko.

Ko took another step toward Grubb, his focus on the black chest in Grubb's arms. Grubb set the chest down by his side, freeing his arms.

"Ye have no reason to distrust me, lad. I'm here on behalf o' Light. Me Celestial testifies to that. The Alveare contains all sorts o' artifacts from both sides. It's important to keep an' study these things, as ye never know when ye might face it out there where the nasties roam. Believe me, lad, I'm protectin' ye an' ye're sister from the nasties. Ye'll thank me one day."

Ko believed Grubb, that Grubb was trying to protect Aileen. Ko's expression indicated he was wrestling with their circumstance and what it meant, for him, for Aileen, for Leo, and for Joan. Ko turned from Grubb to look at Joan, his face wearing a look of uncertainty about what to do, a look that often preceded the look of giving up.

Joan responded to Ko's look. She calmly said, "No," then disappeared.

Grubb looked down by his side to find the Rib Cage holding the ultralight was gone. Ko turned from the spot Joan had warped to see Grubb's discovery. Before Ko could speak, Grubb disappeared as well, warping after Joan. Ko and Aileen were left behind in the Library of Arcs, looking at each other in silence, unsure of what to do.

Joan moved as fast as she could. She had warped to grab the ultralight from Grubb's side and then warped out of the library, out of the mountain completely. She hadn't given much thought to where she was going; she just knew she had to get the ultralight out so Aileen could use it to get to the Aphotic. Joan had taken the cage to the courtyard near the lake's edge. She bent down over the cage, trying to undo its latches. The cage was locked; it required a key. Joan found a boulder nearby and walked toward it with the cage held over head. As she went to throw the cage against the boulder and break the ultralight free, she felt a WHACK!

Grubb had found her and delivered a blow across the back of her head with a wooden training dagger. Joan stumbled, dropping the cage harmlessly to the ground. Grubb grabbed the cage and warped a few paces away from Joan, who was reeling and holding the back of her head, trying to rub the pain away.

Ko arrived with Aileen, too late to play any part in Joan's desperate attempt to release the ultralight.

"I'm sorry, lass, I really am, but I can't let ye do it," said Grubb.

Grubb appeared genuinely sorry for hurting Joan. And the girl's heartbreak, having to let go of her Celestial, her brother, clearly pained him.

When Joan finished tending to the pain pinging the back of her head, she faced Grubb, her teeth gritted in anger and tears streaming from her eyes.

But then, with a deep sigh, Joan's shoulders dropped, and she let go of the anger. She no longer had any hope in saving her brother from a cruel fate. She accepted having failed Leo as a guardian, having failed him as a sister, and that her sweet Leo was gone forever.

CHAPTER TWELVE
VEIL OF THE LAKE

Ko and Aileen approached Joan. They embraced their friend. As Joan sobbed Ko looked across the lake, watching the Veil dance above the water.

Ko understood, as they waited for Leo to perish in the Aphotic, that above all else, the three of them needed hope. A plan, a thought, a dream that the evil consuming Leo could be made right. Ko sought to create that hope. He left Joan in the arms of Aileen, then faced Grubb.

"Say, Grubb, if you were Joan, and your Celestial was trapped in the Aphotic, what would you do?"

"Ko, lad, I know. Ye're right. I'd do anythin' fer me sister, an' I'm really torn, but I know Light, an' I know the Aphotic. It can't be done. Once in the Aphotic, that's it. Think o' ye're sister, Ko, think o' losin' her on top o' losin' Joan's brother, because that's what'll happen if ye're sister reaches the Aphotic. She's not comin' back. The Aphotic is not somethin' to go after. It's a bad place there's no comin' back from," said Grubb.

"If your sister was where Leo is, and you had a long shot at reaching the Aphotic and bringing her back, would you take it?" said Ko.

"Ko … " said Grubb.

"It's a yes or no; you have to be fair in your answer," said Ko.

"Yes, if there were a way, I'd go after me sister in the Aphotic," said Grubb.

"Okay, then you must give Joan a chance, some reason to hope. If you don't, then you're dooming your own Celestial as much as you are Leo," said Ko.

"Ye're right. I owe ye a chance, but I can't do it in good conscience, knowin' ye have no hope in succeedin'. How would I face Light, knowin' I allowed one o' its own, ye're sister, to willingly enter the Aphotic an' be taken ferever?" said Grubb.

"I understand, you need a reason to let us try. A reason to think we have a chance at reaching the Aphotic and saving Leo," said Ko.

Ko paused and let some time pass, letting Grubb think he was trying to come up with a reason. But Ko already knew the reason he'd give to convince Grubb to allow their mission to the Aphotic. Ko had known what to offer Grubb since embracing Joan and watching the Veil dance above the lake.

"What if we beat the Veil and deliver the eyes of the lake to you? Would that be reason enough to let us try the Aphotic? If we bring you the eyes from that podium out there, will you give Aileen back the ultralight, and let us try anything and everything to reach the Aphotic and save Leo?" said Ko.

Grubb turned toward the Veil of the lake, and the small box on the podium, which it guarded. Ko watched as a relief came over Grubb.

Ko knew Grubb understood that the odds of beating the Veil, and stealing the eyes, were not much different than the odds of rescuing a Celestial from the Aphotic. If Grubb accepted this challenge, he'd provide hope to Joan that he himself would expect if in her position. Further, in the very unlikely scenario of Ko or Joan succeeding in stealing the eyes, Grubb would have reason enough to permit a rescue attempt to the Aphotic for Leo, as whoever captured the eyes and beat the Veil of the lake would be deemed an Arc-Iris. It wouldn't be Grubb's place to impede the wishes of another Arc-Iris, a peer equal in authority.

Ko figured that Grubb would take it a step further; he would likely recognize that even if they attempted to travel through a black hole to the Aphotic, the attempt would probably fail, leaving them—or at a minimum, Aileen—unharmed in the universe.

"Okay, lad, ye've got a deal. I'll give each o' ye a turn at the Veil. If either o' ye succeeds in bringin' me the eyes o' that Veil's master, I'll give ye back ye're strange light, an' I won't stop ye from swimmin' through black holes an' gettin' gone ferever in the Aphotic."

Grubb put the Rib Cage full of ultralight on the ground and disappeared from the courtyard in a warp. After a few seconds, Grubb returned with a sash, dagger, and canvas top for Joan.

"Ye'll need these," said Grubb, handing the items to her.

Joan regained her composure as she processed the items from Grubb. While still wearing her jean overalls tucked in her boots, she slipped into the canvas top, which matched what Grubb and Ko wore, and cinched the ties across her chest, pulling the fabric tight. Her angular shoulders and thin frame disappeared under the canvas. She tied the gold sash around her waist and stowed the dagger. After taking a few deep, calming breaths, she stepped alongside Ko, looking across the lake at the Veil silently hovering around the eyes of its former Scant.

"Ko, did he say the eyes of a Scant are out there?" said Joan.

She focused on the small box sitting on the podium in the water.

"Yeah. It's strange, but they took the eyes from a Scant and put them out there. It's a trick on the Veil. It doesn't know any better than to stay near what remains of its master. According to Grubb, if anything gets close to the eyes, the Veil will attack," said Ko.

Grubb stepped alongside the two young Arcs.

"All right, ye each get a turn, an' ye can't help each other out. Who wants to go first?"

"Me," said Joan.

�֍ ✖ ✖

Joan looked at Ko, who nodded in agreement that she could go first. She took a few steps toward the water's edge, then looked back at Ko and Grubb.

"Do you have any advice?" said Joan.

"Don't let it catch ye," said Grubb.

"Good luck," said Ko.

Joan faced the lake. She stared across the placid water, unafraid of being captured by the Veil but terrified of failing Leo. She pushed the terror down. Grit took its place.

Joan ran toward the lake and leaped, flashing from the water's edge, warping high above the valley. She warped again and again, creating a succession of flashes towering in a circular pattern. Each warp provided a step through air, her feet finding nothing solid. Her trajectory in the sky was maintained by moving from one freefalling moment to another, then another, forever keeping the Arc from falling to her death.

Joan circled the Scant eyes, too high to garner the attention of the Veil. With each warp and flash, she looked down from above, stealing a glance at her prey and its defender. Slowly, she began to descend. She tightened the distance between warps, causing the circular path of her descent to funnel toward the eyes. The Veil now sensed Joan's approach. It jerked, snapping into position above the eyes, prepared for the aerial attack. Joan's funneling descent accelerated, soon finding its minimum above the Veil, which hung taut and quivering in anticipation of Joan. Joan stopped the warps, allowing herself to freefall directly above the Veil, gravity now pulling her faster and faster toward the Veil's outstretched fabric.

Moments before, Joan had been high, and the Veil had been a small black dot far below her. Now its black fabric was large and getting larger as she fell. The eyes she sought were now out of sight, hidden behind the fabric of their protector. She had a few split seconds left. The split seconds passed, and the Veil braced for Joan's impact, eager to meet her.

Joan's plummet toward the Veil finished with a flash as she warped to a moment past the Veil. She found herself standing on the podium, with the eyes of the lake before her and the Veil above. She reached to grab the small box. WHAM!

Joan had been too slow. The Veil reacted as fast as Joan had warped past it, snapping to the podium and whipping a blow across Joan's entire body. Joan flew off the podium, skipping across the lake. She flailed as her momentum finished with her crashing under water. Out of breath and bruised with pain, Joan found her bearings and stretched her body upward, gasping for air. Delirious with pain, she broke the surface of the water. She did not find the sky above her but the black fabric of the Veil, hovering and ready to consume her, to finish what it had started. The Veil's fabric bent and curled as it went to wrap Joan. She mustered a breath and warped from the moment, leaving the Veil behind.

Joan landed with a thud on the bank of the lake, near where she had started. She had escaped the wrap of the Veil, barely. Ko, Grubb, and Aileen rushed to her side. They consoled her as she gasped in pain. Joan's lack of air from the Veil's blow was compounded by exhaustion from her warps.

"Joan, you were amazing. Truly fantastic to watch. Don't worry, we still have my turn," said Ko.

Joan didn't respond, other than signaling for Ko to help her up. Once up, Joan stood with her hands on her knees, looking at the ground. Her body still seared in pain, but she had caught her breath. She reached to her side and pulled the dagger from her sash. With a flash, Joan warped back across the water on a direct route to the Veil. Arriving eye level with the Veil of the lake, and within arm's reach, Joan slashed wildly at the black fabric. Joan's dagger found the Veil. WRAP!

Joan lost sight of Eclaireur. She could no longer see or feel the light of Portum Lux. The Veil moved too quickly for the blade to penetrate. It had her now; she had failed again. Joan cringed under the cinch of the Veil's fabric, her body compressing under the squeeze. She went to scream, but her lungs found no air. Suffocation set in. Next came the loss of thought. Joan faded.

Joan awoke. What she lay on was solid. She heard a loud muffled roar. There was still no light; she could only see black. The loud muffled roar became something else.

"Joan! Joan!"

Joan opened her eyes. The black was gone. Lying on her back, she stared up at the sky of Portum Lux. The silhouettes of Aileen, Ko, and Grubb entered her view.

"What were ye thinkin'! A little warnin' would o' been nice!" said Grubb.

Grubb was doubled over and out of breath.

"My turn wasn't done," Joan said flatly.

Her voice was raspy and weak. She didn't feel the need to explain herself further. Grubb, seeing the young Arc was going to make it, stormed off, muttering various curses to himself.

"How'd I get out?" said Joan, referring to her release from the Veil's wrap.

"Grubb. He wrestled you out. It was incredible," started Ko, "In a flash, he warped to where the Veil had you wrapped above the lake, and he just grabbed a hold of the thing. He latched on to one end of the Veil, away from the section of fabric you were in, and started to yank the fabric with one arm while rolling it around his other arm. The Veil gave him a fit, trying to keep you and fight back, with Grubb cursing the entire time. Eventually, the Veil, unable to buck Grubb, began to yield. Grubb broke its spirit in the air and guided it down to the podium. Once on the podium, he continued to roll the fabric around his arm, as if the Veil was a tube of toothpaste, until at last, it spit you out like the last bit of paste. Grubb caught you, tossed the Veil aside, and warped you back to shore. It's taken both you and the Veil a bit to find your bearings again. I wish you could have seen it," said Ko.

"Me too," said Joan.

"Joan, are you okay?" said Aileen.

"Yeah, I'm okay. I'm sorry if I scared you, but I'm fine. And, Ko, I'm sorry I didn't get the eyes. It's not fair to you that I failed. You don't deserve this burden. I want you to know, I don't expect you to return with the eyes, and that it's okay, whatever happens," said Joan.

"I don't mind the burden, and I'm not afraid of the Veil. I actually sort of feel bad for it, which I know is odd. Poor thing is captive to a trick. At least we know it can be tricked," said Ko.

Ko and Aileen helped Joan up for a second time following her bout with the Veil of the lake. The three friends walked to Grubb, who had finished muttering his curses and stood silently near the water's edge, staring out across the lake and its mountains. Aileen and Joan stayed back as Ko stepped forward alongside Grubb.

☀ ☀ ☀

It was Ko's chance to steal the eyes of the lake, something Ko had craved since arriving on the Isle of Eclaireur.

"Ye ready, lad?" said Grubb.

"I think so," said Ko.

"How ye gonna go at it?" said Grubb.

"Well, Joan approached from the sky. I'm not faster than Joan, so there's no sense in trying that. The Veil, once alert to movement, is too fast for me to warp past it. Approaching in an obscure is of no use either, as the Veil will still sense my movement. It seems an obscure is only useful against a Veil if I need to hide and remained perfectly still, which does me no good in trying to steal the eyes," said Ko.

"What ye sayin' is true, lad, but if ye're not gonna warp an' ye're not gonna obscure, what other approach do ye have? Maybe ye're thinkin' o' swimmin' fer it," said Grubb.

"That's kind of what I'm thinking, except I don't plan to get wet," said Ko.

"Now ye've lost me. What are ye getting at?" said Grubb.

"I came across a book in the library, and it gave me an idea I'd like to try," said Ko.

"An' what is that?" said Grubb.

"It involves an approach from beneath the Veil. There's no sense now in explaining further, only trying it. If I return with the eyes, then the book I found and what I've done will be worth discussing. But if I fail, then both the book and my idea won't be worth revisiting. If we're going to reach the Aphotic and save Leo, I must take my turn now. Leo's time is running out," said Ko.

Grubb nodded his head in agreement, signaling for Ko to take his turn at the Veil.

Ko stepped to the water's edge, leaving Grubb and the others behind. He stared across the lake and focused on the small box around which the Veil had resumed its brooding.

His plan was to enter the lake and approach the Veil from under water. This idea was born from a book he had come across in the Library of Arcs, while searching with Aileen for ways to the Aphotic. The book Ko had found was the study of atmospheres forming around planets. Though ancient and unreadable, the book contained pages filled with spherical planets surrounded by layers of lines and squiggles, which suggested the book's atmospherically aimed contents. The diagrams had given Ko an idea for bending time. Ko's plan was to become one of those diagrams, except instead of an atmosphere forming around a planet, he sought to build an atmosphere around himself, allowing him to pass through what would otherwise be an uninhabitable zone.

Ko squared his body with his target and relaxed his mind. He didn't warp or create an obscure. Instead, the young Arc asked time to give him something else. He sought for the air around him to remain with him, moment by moment around his body. The moments in time around Ko responded, anchoring themselves, and the associated air and space, a set distance from him. The result was a bubble, a mini atmosphere, trapped around Ko's person.

Grubb watched, amazed, as Ko and his Sphere entered the lake. With each step, the invisible Sphere moved with Ko. Water was displaced as if a large balloon were being pushed under. Ko's body disappeared beneath the lake's surface, followed by the top of the Sphere being submerged. Ko was gone from sight.

The distance from the shore to the center of the lake was sizeable. Grubb watched both the water and the Veil intently. He wasn't sure how long it would take for Ko to reach the podium while walking across the floor of the lake. He also wasn't sure when or if the Veil would sense that Ko was approaching.

By this time, Aileen and Joan had walked alongside Grubb. The three of them watched silently, waiting for Ko to reappear or for the Veil to shoot underwater, signaling that it was onto Ko. Nothing happened. There was no sign of Ko emerging from the lake, and the Veil continued to float around the podium without a care.

Grubb began to worry. Enough time had passed to where Ko should have reached the podium by now. Grubb's mind raced as he contemplated how deep the lake got near the middle. He knew if Ko lost control of the Sphere, releasing his air, the Arc would be too deep to swim for the surface. If Ko made the mistake of swimming for the surface, instead of warping to safety, he could lose consciousness and drown before Grubb could do anything to help him. Grubb went to warp above the lake, to see if he could locate Ko and confirm if he was okay or in need of help. Before Grubb could move, he saw the Veil jerk. Something had gotten the Veil's attention.

The Veil had stopped moving. It hung frozen, taut and rigid, in response to movement beneath the lake's surface. Zooming to one side of the podium, the Veil paused above the water. It had honed in on Ko's position. The Veil reared back and dove beneath the water. This left the space around the podium empty and motionless, except for ripples from where the Veil had splashed into the lake. Joan and Aileen held their breath. Grubb prepared to dart across the lake, anticipating the Veil would resurface with Ko wrapped in its black fabric.

The three bystanders were astonished at what came next. It wasn't the Veil but Ko, who appeared. He stepped from a warp and onto the podium, then bent down and picked up the box containing the Scant eyes. After he had the eyes in hand, he warped to the shore and stood before Grubb, Joan, and Aileen. Out of breath and smiling, Ko handed the box to Grubb, who took it with a gaping mouth. A few seconds later, the Veil reemerged from the water, near where it had entered. It frantically paced the space around the podium, looking for the eyes of its master.

"How long until it knows they're over here?" said Ko.

"Not long, lad," said Grubb, his mouth still agape.

"Then we'd better put them back, but before we do, can I see the eyes?" said Ko.

Grubb nodded his head and opened the little box. Ko, Joan, Aileen peered inside, where they found a glass jar full of fluid and two eyes floating. In the center of each eye lay a red iris, which still shined as if alive and watching. Grubb could see what went through each of their minds.

Ko felt a thrill seeing the eyes, a triumph mixed with fully grasping the danger of his new reality as an Arc-Iris. Joan felt hope seeing the eyes, knowing the Aphotic was near and that a Scant could be defeated. She hoped Atros would one day have his eyes placed in a box. Aileen felt sad seeing the eyes: she wished it hadn't been the fate of the Scant to whom the eyes once belonged.

Grubb closed the box and warped across the lake. He flashed by the Veil and, while passing the podium, placed the eyes back in their resting place. The Veil jerked to the podium and, instead of giving its attention to Grubb, seemed to coddle the top of the podium where its master had been returned. Almost as soon as he had warped away, Grubb had flashed back and stood among the three friends. Grubb addressed Ko.

"Tell me, lad, how'd ye do it?" said Grubb.

"I created a Sphere and maintained it while moving across the lake's bed, and once arriving at the middle of the lake, I allowed myself to float closer to the surface, but not too close. Just close enough to get the Veil's attention. Once I had it, I pushed myself back deeper, inviting the Veil to give chase. The Veil obliged and came for me. It moved fast, but a hair slower under water. I let the Veil reach me, and even enter the Sphere I had created. It was then that I absolved the Sphere and warped to the top of the podium. The commotion created by the Sphere disappearing, and the water instantly flooding the space left behind, disoriented the Veil just long enough for me to grab the eyes and escape," said Ko.

"Ye know, ye're an Arc-Iris now. It's not a small thin' doin' what ye did, an' ye deserve to be called an Arc-Iris. Everywhere ye go, many will know what ye're capable o', which is anythin'." Grubb turned and addressed Joan, "An,' ye, what ye did was equal to the task. More important than beatin' the Veil, ye showed ye weren't scared. Doin' what ye did tells me that ye no longer have fear, an' the next time ye come face to face with a Scant, it won't be able to hold ye with its gaze."

Grubb reached to shake Joan's hand and then Ko's, signaling his respect for Joan's bravery and for Ko's status as Arc-Iris. Ko and Joan each responded with a sheepish smirk as Grubb's bear paw of a palm engulfed theirs. Both Ko's and Joan's expressions showed relief at knowing they could face Atros without his eyes paralyzing them.

"Tell me now, as a fellow Arc-Iris, how'd ye do that thin', with the bubble an' whatnot goin' underwater? I'd like to learn that trick me-self," said Grubb.

"I got the idea from a book in the library on how atmospheres form around planets. I just did what you taught me and asked time to do something I needed … "

"Ko, we need to go," said Joan.

Joan cut the two Arc-Irises short of any further explanation on how Ko had accomplished stealing the eyes. It would have to wait.

Ko looked at Joan and then back at Grubb.

"Well?" said Ko.

Grubb nodded in acknowledgement of what Joan and Ko were asking of him. Grubb presented the Rib Cage, applied a key to its latch, and opened the trap. Aileen reached inside and grabbed the bag of ultralight. She returned the bag to her side, attaching it to her waist. The ultralight was once again connected with Aileen and ready for her command.

"I can't believe ye're doin' this. I'd ask ye to reconsider, but I don't think ye'll listen," said Grubb.

"No, we have to try," said Joan.

"Don't worry, Grubb, it'll be okay," said Aileen.

"But what o' the two of ye?" said Grubb, referring to Joan and Ko. "Ye might perish in that ultralight as soon as ye leave Portum Lux. How can ye know ye'll make it? Ye know there's nothin' out there in between the worlds an' the light. No air, nothin' ye're bodies need to survive."

"I've thought about that," said Ko. "I'll create a Sphere for Joan and me. A big one. It'll be like our own little world, moving wherever Aileen sends it, keeping us safe, whether it be in space, a black hole, or the Aphotic."

"I have serious doubts as to whether that'll work, but it doesn't matter now. I can tell ye're minds are made up. I wish ye the best, truly. I hope to see the three o' ye again, an' if I don't, I'll be deeply saddened. Even more, I hope the three 'o ye find Leo an' bring him back to this side o' the Aphotic. Joan, ye're one brave Arc, an' ye've done well by ye're Celestial, no matter what happens next."

Joan gave a quick nod in response to Grubb, then turned to Aileen and Ko.

"All right, let's go. Aileen, are you ready? Ko, can you create the Sphere?" said Joan.

They each nodded in response.

"Grubb, you may want to give this a little space," said Ko.

Grubb obliged, warping back toward the Alveare, removing himself from the footprint of the Sphere Ko was preparing to create.

The three friends came together, shoulder to shoulder, by the lake of Eclaireur. Ko focused, creating a large Sphere to encapsulate Joan and himself, providing everything they needed to survive the journey. Aileen didn't need the protection of the Sphere, now that she knew how to move as a quantum beam.

With the Sphere created, trapping a portion of Portum Lux air and pressure, Ko looked at Aileen.

"So, how exactly is this going to happen?" said Ko.

"Well, I'm going to join with the ultralight, wrap you and Joan in a beam, and aim us at the heart of a black hole. After that, your guess is as good as mine," said Aileen.

"How do you know what black hole to aim at?" said Joan. "Sordara said Atros would keep Leo somewhere he couldn't be found and that the Aphotic is infinite and incomprehensible. There are countless black holes in existence. How do we know which black hole will get us close to where Atros is keeping Leo?"

"I saw one when I visited Leo's galaxy. I'm going to aim for that one. I feel like it'll take us where we need to go," said Aileen.

In stark contrast to the danger they were facing, Aileen's voice remained childlike, innocent and without fear.

"Okay. That works for me. Before we go, let's remember that, wherever we go, and whatever we face, the three of us are to stay close to one another. Agreed?" said Ko.

"Agreed," said Joan.

"Okay, Aileen, create whatever we're about to ride, and let's go. What do you call it?" said Ko.

"An ultralight beam," said Aileen, her face scrunching into a smile.

Aileen called the ultralight out. Tiny and bright, the ultralight bled into the valley. Aileen's body dissolved into quantum particles and joined with the ultralight, the specks of ultralight coming together with Aileen to encapsulate Ko's Sphere, which contained him and Joan.

The Sphere of ultralight flashed from the surface of Portum Lux and stretched into an ultralight beam. The beam left Portum Lux and disappeared into the depths of the universe, on course for a black hole in Leo's galaxy, and ultimately the Aphotic.

From Grubb's point of view on Portum Lux, the beam appeared and disappeared, leaving behind a thin line of light, which chased its beginning up and into the blackness of space.

CHAPTER THIRTEEN
APHOTIC

The Aphotic did not appear different than any other dark place; that is, a truly dark place, completely absent of light. Without light, it could not be gauged whether the Aphotic was small, like a dark room with walls, or infinite, with never ending clear space to run through without fear of hitting anything. Though the Aphotic did not appear different than other truly dark places found in the universe, it did *feel* different, both in touch and in the intangible sense that tells the mind that it is somewhere it really ought not to be.

Having carried the three friends safely through the black hole, Aileen's ultralight now spread before the three friends, providing the trio with their first sight of the Aphotic. They found themselves standing on what felt like solid ground. But the black mossy substance beneath their feet lacked traction. Looking across what the ultralight revealed, they saw an unending expanse, with a perfectly flat ground, and no end to the black space above. The only sounds they could detect came from their own steps and what seemed to be a dull, unvarying wind.

Aileen motioned for the ultralight to return to her. It obeyed, the multitude of tiny light flakes converging to the young Celestial. The ultralight settled in a cluster next to Aileen. She leaned into the cluster and whispered, "Take us to Leo, and don't be too bright."

Joan and Ko watched as the cluster of ultralight dimmed to a hazy glow. Once dimmed, the cluster seemed to explode, with each flake of light shooting off in a different direction across the Aphotic. The ultralight disappeared into the black of the Aphotic, with only one bead of ultralight staying behind to provide the three friends with light enough to see one another. Joan, Ko, and Aileen crowded together, the darkness around them appearing much closer than moments before. They waited silently, Ko and Joan each in their thoughts and anxious about what would come next, straining their eyes for any movement that might reveal itself to be a Scant, or its Veil.

Not long passed before the ultralight returned, though it did not return to Aileen in the same manner it had left. Instead of clustering around Aileen, the ultralight, each flake returning from a different corner of the Aphotic, created a line stretching far across the mossy black surface. The message was clear: for Ko, Joan, and Aileen to follow the trail created by the ultralight.

They began to follow the path, walking at first, with each flake of ultralight distanced from the next, such that as soon as reaching one flake of ultralight, the next flake was just close enough for the three friends to see. They realized, after reaching the first flake of ultralight, that the trail was long, with a great distance spread from one flake to the next.

"This is going to take too long. We won't get to him in time if we walk," said Joan.

They approached and stood around the first flake of ultralight in the trail. They gazed deep into the dark where the next marker of the trail glowed dimly.

"Agreed. We need to warp. Stand close," said Ko.

He pulled Joan and Aileen close, ensuring that with each warp the three stayed together within the Sphere he still maintained. The trio warped along the trail of ultralight. Aileen pocketed each flake as they went. The markers of the trail disappeared quickly as they moved through the Aphotic, seeking the end of a trail they hoped led to Leo.

Joan's eyes strained after every warp, looking forward to the next glow in hopes that it would reveal Leo. Each warp only took a moment, but each moment felt like an eternity to Joan. She wanted to find Leo, to touch him and tell him it was going to be all right. Each warp brought another flake of ultralight, and no sign of Leo.

The black mossy floor of the Aphotic, and the fathomless corners of the dark around Joan, seemed to bend and twist. Joan felt as though a cold from the emptiness was penetrating and closing in around them. She began to second guess the ultralight. Sordara had told her no other being, besides Dark itself, knew the folds and layers of the Aphotic better than Atros, that Joan would "never find" where Atros had hidden Leo. With each warp deeper into the Aphotic, Sordara's words echoed louder and louder in Joan's head. Her mind raced: what if Sordara had revealed black holes on purpose, as a trick for them to travel to the Aphotic and deliver Aileen into the hands of Atros? Joan glanced quickly behind her, back to where they had come. All she could see was black. She panicked at not seeing a way back to where they had come, a way back to Portum Lux where Aileen would be safe.

Joan looked forward and tried to focus on what remained of the ultralight trail. She told herself it would be okay, that they would find Leo and find a way out. Her internal persuasions felt empty and untrue. She lost focus. She was now convinced that the black depths of the Aphotic were indeed moving. Sordara was right, Joan thought, she'd never find Leo, and Light Reapers were the ones who "do the finding." Joan reached to grab Ko and stop him, to tell him they needed to turn around and go back for Aileen's sake.

"Look!" said Aileen.

Joan turned her attention from the dark of the Aphotic and looked forward. Up ahead, along the trail of ultralight, the dim breadcrumbs led to a bright finish.

Ko accelerated before Joan or Aileen could say more. Within a matter of moments, Ko had warped them a few feet from where the trail of ultralight ended. The three friends struggled to process what they found.

A body lay motionless before them, wrapped in the fabric of the Aphotic. It was Leo. The remainder of the ultralight, not pocketed by Aileen along the trail, clustered and swarmed the silhouette of Leo's body in an embrace. The embrace was aimed to loosen the fabric of the Aphotic, which strewed from the mossy floor as a tightly sewn cocoon around the young Celestial. The ultralight moved frantically around Leo's concealed body.

Joan threw herself by Leo's side, brushing the ultralight out of the way. She tore and ripped at the black fabric, each tear revealing another layer of black. Gasping and in tears, Joan shred the mossy threads around her brother. Ko and Aileen dropped to their knees and joined the effort, with the ultralight filling in any gaps left by the three. Thread by thread, the grasp of the Aphotic was undone.

With the black cocoon torn, Joan's eyes found what she had sought so intently, the one who had been taken from her. She pulled Leo into her arms, squeezing his lifeless body tight, whispering into his ear, "Here I am, here I am."

Leo's face was handsome but faint. He appeared to be in a deep slumber. His light hair was matted. Thin eyebrows arched above his closed eyes. And his lips were slightly parted. He didn't respond to Joan. His body lay limp, his strength and consciousness drained by the Aphotic. Joan continued to whisper and embrace, seeking some sort of response showing he was still there.

Aileen, recognizing the effect of Leo's extensive isolation in the Aphotic, released all the ultralight. The flakes moved toward Joan and Leo, clustering and creating a cover for the two. Ko and Aileen took a step back as the image of Joan holding Leo disappeared under a blanket of ultralight. A dimming, then brightening, glow oscillated across the silhouette of Joan and Leo buried within the ultralight.

A few moments passed before the ultralight dispersed, breaking into tiny flakes and slowly floating away. Ko and Aileen gazed upon what the ultralight had left behind, Joan holding her brother, who held her gaze with open eyes.

"Joan," said Leo, his voice weak.

"There you are," said Joan, feeling Leo's frail embrace.

Ko and Aileen broke out in tears laced with laughter, the sight of their friend's joy an emotion too overwhelming to contain.

Despair had been replaced with relief. Their quest was complete. Joan allowed herself to enjoy a few moments basking in the relief of seeing her brother again. But she soon recognized the relief as an indulgence, and her attention shifted to focus on the four of them exiting the Aphotic and returning to Portum Lux immediately.

"Aileen," said Joan, "How do we get out of here? Can you take us back through the black hole?"

"It should be as simple as how we entered. I'll form an ultralight beam. It will take us back the way we came, back through the black hole, and back to Portum Lux," said Aileen.

"What is Portum Lux?" said Leo, his words barely audible.

"Don't speak. We'll explain later; there's a lot to show you once we're back on the other side," said Joan, who then turned from Leo to Aileen. "Aileen, do it. Let's get out of here."

"Okay," said Aileen.

Aileen turned to Ko.

"Are you ready?" said Aileen.

Ko nodded yes, maintaining his focus on the Sphere, which protected him and Joan.

Aileen, just as she had done on Portum Lux, called the ultralight. Like before, the ultralight spread itself evenly around the four, taking up a vast presence within the Aphotic. Aileen closed her eyes and initiated joining her being with the ultralight. The ultralight beam began to form, joining with Aileen and creating a ball of light around Ko's Sphere, which would, in moments, stretch into a beam flashing and leave the Aphotic behind.

But, before Aileen could complete the beam, there was a disruption from the depths of the Aphotic. Aileen felt the disturbance in her connection with the ultralight. Searching her feelings, she found some of the ultralight had suddenly gone missing. She had felt every ounce of ultralight in one moment, and in the next moment, a small amount was gone and out of her reach. Aileen's heart jumped, and she opened her eyes as she felt a rapid severance with a great volume of ultralight.

Ko and Joan looked at Aileen with puzzled expressions, confused as to why Aileen had halted the ultralight beam. They followed Aileen's gaze, which was darting in all directions upward and outward into the Aphotic.

What they saw terrified them. The ultralight was disappearing. The outermost flakes of ultralight were going dark. The rolling blackout quickly converged on Ko, Joan, Aileen, and Leo. Aileen called for what ultralight remained to return to her, but it was too late, and the closest of flakes went out before reaching her. The black of the Aphotic, and blindness, was all that remained around the four of them.

Joan helped Leo to his feet. Ko and Aileen drew close to Joan and Leo, reaching out in the dark to find each other. The four of them clasped arms around one another, holding tightly and afraid to let go.

"Where did the ultralight go?" whispered Ko.

"Dark took it," sounded a familiar voice from the black of the Aphotic.

The voice belonged to Atros.

Ko and Joan jerked to face toward Atros's voice, pushing Aileen and Leo behind them. Joan wordlessly handed Leo into Aileen's arms, who did her best to hold him up. Ko and Joan drew the daggers from their sashes, each brandishing their blades in the dark, and leaned in the direction from which Atros's voice had come. They each kept an arm stretched behind them so as not to lose contact with Aileen and Leo.

"Aileen, can you get the ultralight back? We need to beam out of here immediately," said Ko, whispering over his shoulder.

"No. I can't feel it. It's like when Grubb put it in that cage. The ultralight can't hear or feel me, and I can't feel it. Ko, I don't feel good. I need to lay down," said Aileen.

Aileen lowered Leo to the ground, then lay next to him. The cold moss of the Aphotic floor embraced the two Celestials. Ko turned and knelt beside his sister. "Aileen, what's wrong?" His voice was earnest, the fear for his sister's well-being gripping him. Aileen didn't respond. Ko strained his eyes against the dark for a glimpse of Aileen's face. Though her face was inches from his, Ko could only see black. "Aileen? Aileen!" repeated Ko as he grasped and shook her shoulders. Still, Aileen did not respond.

"She belongs to the Aphotic now," interrupted Atros, hoarsely echoing from somewhere in the dark. "What a strange thing for you to do. To bring your Celestial to the Aphotic. Surely, throughout the history of time, such a thing has never occurred. To escort your little sister, a treasure of Light, whom, as an Arc, you are charged to protect above all else, from perfect safety to the very place that guarantees her destruction. What's the phrase you use on Earth—roll over in a grave? Yes, that's it. Your parents would roll over in their graves if they knew what you've done."

Ko's body visibly shook in a cringe as Atros spoke.

"Though, your parents don't have graves to roll over in. They weren't buried at all. They simply vanished here, in the nothingness of the Aphotic. What's interesting about your parents, Ko, is that they brought a chain of light with them. The light meant they had to watch as the other faded. They didn't get to experience the mercy of the Aphotic, the black that keeps you from seeing your loved ones suffer. Let me remove that mercy for you. I want you to see the Aphotic taking your sister as you perish, watching and knowing that she will be here alone for some time after you're gone, suffering until she's been put out, entering the forever never phase of existence. So, as it was once said, let there be light."

The Aphotic responded to Atros, releasing a red phosphorous glow from its mossy floor. It wasn't light but soft neon lumens seeping from the flesh of the Aphotic.

Ko's and Joan's eyes adjusted to the red glow. They could now make out Atros's slender figure, standing far off, just outside Ko's Sphere, which continued to sustain Ko and Joan in the Aphotic. Both Ko and Joan stole a glance at Leo and Aileen, each now unconscious on the floor of the Aphotic.

"Before we continue, you will answer some questions I have. How did you reach the Aphotic? What you see around you is a dimension of existence to which beings should not be able to travel, except through the Veil of a Scant," said Atros.

Ko and Joan remained silent.

"Very well. I'll speculate. There are no other Scants here except for me. That means you didn't receive assistance from a traitor, moved to abandon Dark for Light. Such treason would be harder to believe than you being here at all. That leaves black holes. I can imagine you learning about the nature of black holes. How black holes are cosmic tears in the universe that act as portals to the Aphotic. However, knowledge of black holes is not enough to travel through one. You would have needed help. Only Light itself could provide such help. Light, that's it! The light I took from you, those tiny specks. It helped you get here, did it not?"

Ko and Joan glanced at each other but refused to respond to Atros. They each held tightly to the hilts of their daggers.

"I'll let it go, for now. I know those specks of light are how you reached the Aphotic. Moving on, let me ask you another question.

I'll give you one more chance to answer without me needing to pry it out of you. What else have you brought with you?" said Atros.

Atros waved his hand, motioning to Ko's Sphere, just outside of which Atros stood.

Ko saw an opportunity for a bluff.

"It's a Sphere, something no Scant has seen before. Powerful enough to pass through a black hole. Though, as a Light Reaper I'm sure it wouldn't harm you. Why don't you step inside, so we can find out?" said Ko.

Ko knew it was just atmosphere, harmless air and temperature, which would do no harm to Atros. Ko hoped Atros would hesitate to approach, buying him and Joan more time to think of a way to escape.

"A Sphere, powerful enough to pass through a black hole. I suppose I should be afraid. Though, I see you are no longer afraid. My gaze has been searching, but it has found no fear in your hearts with which to bind you. Your bravery is most inspiring. So much so that I feel the need to act myself, and conquer my fears," Atros finished, dryly.

Atros then stepped into Ko's Sphere without hesitation and without fear.

Joan shot Ko a cynical look.

"It was worth a shot," said Ko.

"I know from where this came," quipped Atros, referring to what now surrounded his body. "Portum Lux. What a repulsive nostalgia one experiences. It's an unforgettable smell, disgusting. I think I understand the mechanics, Ko, of how you brought this here, and why. It's quite brilliant of you, very imaginative. It's a shame your abilities as an Arc will end here in the Aphotic. If you lived past the next few moments, you certainly would have reached Arc-Iris."

"He is an Arc-Iris," snapped Joan. She looked at Ko. "One of us has to bury a dagger in his chest."

"Agreed. Let's go," said Ko.

The two Arcs broke into action with Atros as their target. Each warped near the Light Reaper, staggering their approach to appear random as they closed in. Atros remained unmoved by the advance, minus one or two twitches in anticipation of Ko and Joan.

Ko arrived first, now standing within striking distance of the Light Reaper. Ko lunged at Atros, his dagger aimed for the heart. An instant later, Joan arrived on the opposite side of Atros. Joan's warp was more aggressively targeted. She placed her body within inches of Atros, so no lunge would be needed. She went to sink her dagger in Atros's back.

The young Arcs didn't see the impact coming. From the depths of the Aphotic, Atros's Veil arrived. Ko's lunge and Joan's stab never found the slender figure of the tall Light Reaper. Instead, they each received a blow from Atros's Veil, which threw them across the Aphotic moss and back toward where they had started.

Ko, dazed, lost focus. In turn, the Sphere from Portum Lux began to dissipate. Ko's mind jerked back to the moment, and he regained control over what remained of the Sphere, which was a little smaller now than a moment before.

Joan and Ko each recovered to their feet and faced Atros, who stood with a smug expression, his massive Veil now affectionately circling above its master.

Gasping from the blow, Joan looked back at Leo, still unconscious and running out of time. Leo's body looked lifeless, gray and without color. The work of the Aphotic was almost complete. Joan's blood boiled with anger. Her anger shifted focus from Atros to his Veil, the source of Atros's power and ultimately the object obstructing their escape. Joan warped again, leaving Ko behind. Her advance mirrored her first attempt. The Veil hovered above its master, ready to repel Joan no matter what side of Atros she attacked, though Joan wasn't aiming for Atros this time. At the last moment, she wrinkled her final warp high above Atros and across the Veil instead.

Joan warped back to Ko's side. Ko looked from Joan back to Atros, who seemed confused about what had just happened. A small piece of black fabric floated down near Atros, who reached out with an outstretched hand and snared the fabric before it could touch the ground. Atros looked upward, where his Veil now writhed in pain. Its rectangular shape was now missing a corner, which Joan's dagger had severed. Joan looked at Ko.

"Forget about Atros. Go for the Veil; without it, Atros is nothing," said Joan.

Joan disappeared from Ko's side into a warp, once again aiming her dagger for Atros's Veil. Ko wasted no time following suit. Both Arcs warped all around Atros's towering Veil, each taking swipes and cuts high above before retreating to safety.

The Veil and Atros were caught off guard and slow to react at first. Atros, stuck to the floor of the Aphotic and watching what was happening above him, called out to his Veil in a panic, "Destroy them!"

The Veil responded, snapping back and forth after the young Arcs. A whirlwind of flashes ensued, with the black fabric of the great Veil becoming entangled with the outlines of Ko and Joan, their daggers reflecting the red glow of the Aphotic. A series of blows landed, and the commotion stopped. Atros peered into the space above, which now appeared to be empty. He grinned, as the lack of movement seemed to signal the young Arcs had been neutralized.

"Come to me," said Atros.

His request was directed upward into the black, seeking for his Veil to return to his side. Moments passed as nothing happened, and there was only silence. Atros's grin disappeared.

The red glow of the Aphotic revealed small pieces of fabric floating down from above. Atros watched in disbelief as the shreds of his Veil fell lifelessly around him. His Veil had been destroyed, carved to pieces by the two young Arcs, whom Atros now saw standing across the Aphotic, each having survived the battle with his Veil.

Ko and Joan had returned to Leo and Aileen, each Arc standing with their hands on their knees, gasping for breath. Their bodies throbbed from blows landed by Atros's Veil, the impacts already bruising, with some showing cuts and the slow trickle of blood. Joan's face sported a large gash across her cheek, while Ko's face was blanketed with lacerations from the Veil's strikes. They didn't feel the pain, only pleasure at watching the pieces of black fabric fall around Atros. Once they gained their bearings Ko and Joan straightened, standing at their full height and staring across the red of the Aphotic toward the astounded Light Reaper, who now stood defenseless.

"If you give us the ultralight back, and let us leave, we'll let you live," said Ko.

Atros didn't respond at first. He seemed stuck somewhere, struggling to see what was before him. The red in his eyes slowly returned its focus to the two Arcs. His eyes burned across the

Aphotic. He began to smile. The smile became a chuckle. The chuckle turned to laughter, and the laughter bled into a roaring crow. Gaining his composure, he spoke, "You're no different than your parents, just as foolish. Do you not see me? Am I not standing here before you? Do you not see where you are? Look around you!"

Atros motioned violently to the surrounding darkness of the Aphotic.

Ko and Joan's eyes drifted from Atros to the periphery. The black depths of the Aphotic seemed to shift and move. They heard a loud and long tear from the dark, like the curtain of a stage being torn from top to bottom. The sound was followed by a roaring commotion in the space above them. The source of the commotion became visible against the red glow of the Aphotic floor. Another Veil settled above Atros, replacing the one Joan and Ko had destroyed.

Ko and Joan looked at each other in desperation. They could see it in one another's eyes. They were defeated. Even if they defeated another Veil, another would come. Even if they killed Atros, they wouldn't get the ultralight back from the Aphotic. They'd never see Portum Lux again, and both of their beloved Celestials would be doomed, along with their galaxies. Leo and Aileen were already fainter than moments before, their beings having fallen further into the pale and restless sleep of the Aphotic.

Ko and Joan stepped toward one another and leaned into an embrace, partly consoling and partly in farewell. They hugged in silence for a few seconds. Ko went to step away, but Joan stopped Ko's motion and pulled him back to her, landing her lips on his. The kiss was brief.

Joan pulled away from Ko and kneeled beside Leo. Ko did the same, kneeling next to Aileen. They embraced their sleeping Celestials in a final good-bye, and after their whispers, they stood, once again facing the Light Reaper who had haunted them from the beginning.

"Joan, I'm very thankful to have known you," said Ko.

"And, me you. Are you ready?" said Joan.

"Yes," said Ko.

The two Arcs flashed across the Aphotic, daggers in hand. They sought to finish Atros, to ensure that if they died, he went with them. The Light Reaper stood calmly, watching as his new Veil engaged with the two Arcs. A flicker of warps burst around the black fabric of the Veil, each warp accompanied by the streak of a dagger swiping at the Veil. As before, they struck the Veil, cutting and tearing it one strike at a time. With the Veil on the defensive, Ko saw an opportunity, a window to break from the Veil and attack Atros. Ko landed a blow on one end of the Veil, while Joan sliced elsewhere. Ko pulled his dagger from the fabric and warped to Atros, dagger raised. He landed and swung the dagger at the defenseless Light Reaper.

His momentum was halted by the shifty Scant, who, with a simple step, had avoided Ko's dagger and clamped down on Ko's outstretched arm, holding the fatigued Arc in a compromising position. With his other hand, Atros delivered a blow across Ko's face, causing Ko to drop his dagger. Atros then gave a push, sending Ko backward, the thrust of the momentum causing Ko to trip and roll across the mossy ground. Atros picked up Ko's dagger and threw it into the depths of the Aphotic, out of the red glow and into the blackness.

Ko looked up from the Aphotic floor to find Joan still battling the Veil, though now on the defensive without his assistance. He watched in agony as the Veil snapped a devastating blow across Joan. Her body went limp, and her dagger fell from her hand. Ko flashed in a warp to Joan, grabbing her in midair as she began to fall. Before he could warp back down to safety, the Veil had them. Its black fabric wrapped around them and held them suspended. With a crack, the Veil whipped the two Arcs downward. Ko and Joan landed with a thud on the Aphotic floor.

☀ ☀ ☀

Atros walked toward the motionless Arcs. His newly acquired Veil, mildly tattered from the fight, hovered just above Ko and Joan. The edges of it draped and brushed across their bodies as Atros approached. Stepping near, Atros looked down at the unconscious Arcs, then at the black fabric of the Veil. He examined the damage done to the fabric, quipping, "That's okay; we can fix that."

Beyond the holes in his new Veil, Atros noticed something else, the dissipation of Ko's Sphere. Slowly, the web of moments crumbled, no longer maintained by the now unconscious Ko. Atros watched as the last of the Portum Lux atmosphere disappeared.

Returning his focus to Ko and Joan, Atros took pleasure watching their bodies succumb to the Aphotic, the lack of air forcing them to wake up. Atros stood over Ko and Joan as their eyes opened, their faces contorting silently into expressions revealing the torture their bodies began to experience.

Cruelly, Atros proceeded to taunt the suffering Arcs, "I know how this finishes, Ko. I watched as your parents suffered the same end. As with them, unfortunately, your pain won't last much longer. Just a little more and you'll be what your parents are, gone. It's amazing, really, at how peculiar you are. Peculiar like your parents. Like them, you brought light to the Aphotic, a place where light doesn't exist. Your father bound himself to your mother with that chain of light. It was as if he thought that light would protect them in the Aphotic. What a fool. They lasted a few minutes before dying. After your parents were gone, I cast the chain away. I watched its glowing strands float off, becoming smaller and smaller, until the light disappeared against the black of the Aphotic. Your father's final words to me, before I brought him to the Aphotic, were, 'We'll see.' If only he were here to see, he would see how much his son truly takes after him, a … "

Atros abandoned what he was saying as a flicker caught the corner of his eye. He turned away from the fading Arcs to find a strange and unexpected sight, which deeply puzzled the Light Reaper.

Aileen was standing, the chain of light from her parents in her hands. The chain was made of ultralight, and Atros was too late.

The shape of Aileen's body disappeared into a beam. The ultralight beam spread across the Aphotic. Atros frantically moved to avoid its path. An elongated pause of the enormous beam illuminated the Aphotic, casting a purple haze into the black depths. Its hesitation complete, the ultralight beam collapsed in on itself, vanishing, darkness once again residing in every corner of the Aphotic.

Atros searched frantically, but there was no one to find. He was alone. His prey had escaped. He groaned in agony, knowing he had failed to stop the first ever breach of the Aphotic, the first ever rescue of a Celestial. In the history of existence, no being of Light, especially a Celestial, had ever escaped from the Aphotic.

Atros's agony began to lift, but only to make room for another sensation. The Light Reaper felt a dread creeping into his being. Atros realized that Dark knew what had happened.

CHAPTER FOURTEEN
STRANGER

Ko awoke. His eyes adjusted to the light. The Aphotic was gone. He was somewhere else now. The ceiling of a small room came into focus. Turning his head from side to side, he found himself in a bed, neatly tucked beneath white covers. Ko pushed the covers away and slowly sat up. The movement brought pain as his bruised body responded. He groaned, struggling to hold himself upright. Taking in the rest of the room, he saw he wasn't alone. Sitting in a corner of the room was Sam, slumped and asleep, with a steady snore rattling his mustache.

"Sam?"

The steward of Tourlitis stirred, his eyes blinking open. His posture straightened in the chair. After a series of snorts and throat-clearing coughs, he found his bearings and his voice.

"Ko! There you are. Finally awake. How do you feel?"

"I feel, um, sore. Where are we?"

"You're back on Portum Lux. Specifically, back on Tourlitis."

"What happened? The last thing I remember is Atros and then light. I thought it was the end. I thought we were gone. Is this real?"

"Yes, this is real, and it would have been the end had it not been for your parents, and of course, your wonderful sister. She is quite something, your sister. She found something in the Aphotic your parents had left for her to find, a chain of light. Your sister used it to wrap you up, along with the others, in some sort of beam, which against all odds, brought you safely back from the Aphotic. It's astounding, really. Never in history has such a thing been heard of, escaping from the Aphotic. In time, news of the feat will spread throughout the universe. Such a blow to Dark needs to be known by all."

"The others—you mean, Joan, Leo, and Aileen. Are they safe? Where is Aileen?"

"They are all safe and here with you on Tourlitis. In fact, they are a few rooms over. I asked them to let you rest and to let me be the first to speak with you once you were awake. Joan was worse off than you when the four of you arrived, but apparently, she's tougher than you. She didn't need much rest before she was up and walking again. You, however, have been unconscious for days. No matter, you are back with us now."

Ko's thoughts jumped back to his parents. He had felt it since Stono, that his parents were gone. He had tried to not allow hope, but he had still maintained a little hope up until they met Atros in the Aphotic. Sam said his parents had left ultralight for them in the Aphotic. He knew if they had left something for them in the Aphotic, then they had embraced their fate in Stono, and were truly gone.

"Sam, my parents, what does it mean? I know they're gone, but what happened to us in the Aphotic? You said my parents provided ultralight for Aileen ... how?"

"I must say, I still don't fully understand how you reached the Aphotic, how you survived, and how you returned. It's not a stretch for the feat to be considered impossible, but here you are regardless. From talking with your cohorts, I've gathered that the chain of light your parents had bound themselves together with, when they were taken by Atros, was some form of ultralight they had managed to create on their own. The mystics and romantics would say that a form of love allowed them to create it. That may be true, but who is to say for certain? No matter. Your parents somehow knew what they were doing. The chain of ultralight they had created in Stono persisted in the Aphotic, even after your parents perished. Further, that chain of ultralight found its way to your sister at exactly the right moment necessary for an improbable escape. Your sister didn't allow Atros time to react. She set her beam in motion, and here you all are, safe."

"What about you, Sam? Where have you been?"

"As planned, I went with Joan to Mouro, assisting her with Sordara, but I had to leave Mouro and hold court with an unexpected visitor to Portum Lux. Someone who, like the three of you when you first arrived here, was seeking help."

"Were you able to help the visitor?"

"Time will tell."

"Is the visitor still here on Tourlitis?"

"No, the visitor left. Her stay was short. I gave her what guidance I could, then she went on her way."

"Was she like us? Has another Celestial been taken to the Aphotic?"

"No, thank goodness. She was an Arc traveling by herself. Her Celestial is no longer a Nebula and has in fact been a Quasar for some time. Of course, Quasar Celestials are safe from the Aphotic, so I told her there was nothing to worry about. She refused to listen and insisted her Celestial and its galaxy were in danger, at risk of being taken by Dark. She left not long before the four of you returned from the Aphotic."

"Where did she go, this Arc?"

"Oddly enough, she is heading for your Earth."

"That's strange."

"It is stranger than you know; your two friends actually know her quite well."

Ko thought for a moment.

"You mean, the visiting Arc was Stranger? Joan and Leo's guardian?"

"That's right. Of course, Stranger is not her given name, though I'm sure she would still respond to that calling," said Sam.

Ko's mind raced. Stranger's book was what had brought them to Portum Lux. That book had his family's name and address in it. Stranger had to have known his parents. If he could find her, then maybe Stranger could answer questions about his family's past. Then Ko thought about his friends.

"Have you told Joan and Leo that she was here?" said Ko.

"I have not."

"Why not?"

"I'm afraid that once I tell Joan about Stranger, she'll be at it again, ready to bounce around the universe, chasing danger and darkness. The four of you have been through enough. Leo and Joan deserve to enjoy being reunited. You and Aileen still need time to process everything that has happened. Not very long ago, you didn't know the true nature of your existence, of who you and your sister really were. So, let's keep Stranger a secret between you and me for a little while. There's no rush to tell Joan and Leo, and I expect that after some rest and being still for a while, we will find the right moment."

"Does Stranger know about Joan and Leo?"

"She does. It took us a little bit to make the connection, me connecting that she was the guardian from Joan and Leo's story, and her connecting that Leo was the captured Celestial and Joan one of the Arcs trying to save him in the story I shared with her. She was heartbroken when she learned of Leo's fate, and that Joan had gone into the Aphotic after him. Stranger blamed herself. Of course, she could have never imagined that Joan and Leo would return from the Aphotic. Stranger left Portum Lux under the impression that Leo and Joan were gone for good. I imagine Stranger will be quite overwhelmed when she learns what you've done in the Aphotic, and that both Leo and Joan are safe."

"Sam, you said Stranger was worried about her Celestial, even though her Celestial is a Quasar. Why was she worried?"

"You don't need to concern yourself—"

"Sam, it's fine, I was in the Aphotic with a Light Reaper. I can handle it. And if something is going to threaten Aileen once she's a Quasar, then I need to know about it."

"Very well, as long as this stays between you and me. When I say we can tell the others about Stranger, we'll tell them everything. Agreed?"

"Agreed."

"Good. The story is as follows then. When Stranger saved Joan and Leo from Atros the first time, she warped herself with Atros to a remote corner of the universe seldom traveled. Stranger had traveled this part of the universe before and knew it quite well, while Atros did not. As Stranger tells it, she escaped from Atros, eluding him as he sought to capture her. Stranger warped across worlds, with Atros in pursuit. Eventually, she lost Atros, who gave up the chase. Instead of continuing to pursue Stranger, Atros resolved to return to Earth in hopes of finding Joan and Leo once again. Being the cunning Arc that she is, Stranger doubled back and kept tabs on his movements. She knew Atros would return for Joan and Leo. However, while tracking Atros, she came across a dark occurrence in the universe. It's silly, really ...."

Sam paused, appearing unsure of whether to continue. Ko listened closely as Sam began muttering under his breath. Ko picked up a "I'm confident she's wrong ..." and then a "she doesn't know what she saw ...", but on the whole, Ko was unable to follow Sam's muffled soliloquy.

"Sam, what did she find?"

"Well, according to Stranger, an entire Quasar galaxy is missing. One that belonged to a Quasar Celestial she knew well. I told her she had to be mistaken. Either her bearings were backward, and she wasn't where she thought she was, or the galaxy she was looking for had simply moved. You know, objects in the universe are not stationary. It's very possible, if enough time passes, for a galaxy to move great distances or for relativity to change."

"What was her response to your theories? You know, about how she may have lost her bearings, or how the Quasar galaxy may have moved from where she thought it had been?"

"She insisted the galaxy was truly gone, citing that she had looked all over, twice verifying her bearings and the location where the missing galaxy belonged."

"Did she say anything else?"

"Only that she had sensed a deep evil where she believed the galaxy had once been, an 'unseeable threat sulking nearby' were her exact words."

Ko and Sam sat silently for a few minutes, each pondering the warning that was Stranger's story.

"Why did Stranger go to Earth?" said Ko.

"That's where she believes her Celestial is. She wants to find her Celestial in case there's a real threat to her Celestial's well-being."

"Why would her Celestial be on Earth? I thought a Quasar could be anywhere in the universe, wherever light goes?"

"That's true."

"Then why does Stranger think her Celestial is on Earth?"

"Stranger knows her brother best, and Stranger believes she'll find her brother in his galaxy."

"In his galaxy … "

Ko's voice trailed off as he grasped what it meant. Stranger's brother was the Milky Way, the galaxy of his home.

"Sam, if Stranger is right, and Quasars are in danger, and something happened to her brother, then…"

Ko's voice trailed off again. Sam let a few seconds pass before answering the question Ko had started to ask.

"Yes, that's right. Your world would be destroyed. Your sun would stop burning. There'd be no light to sustain your Earth."

"Sam—"

"Boy, I know what you're thinking, and what you're going to say, but I assure you there's nothing to worry about. Stranger's brother is a Quasar. The Milky Way is a Quasar. It is out of Dark's reach and perpetually connected with Light."

"But, Sam—"

Sam stood from his chair, talking faster and louder.

"I won't hear anymore. The notion is ridiculous. It's impossible for Dark to capture and destroy a Quasar."

"But, Sam, you said it was impossible for us to return from the Aphotic. What if this is the same? What if there is a way for Quasars to be captured, even extinguished?"

Flustered, Sam began to respond, but he was stopped by a knock at the door, followed by Aileen's muffled voice coming through the door. "Sam, can we come in? I can hear you talking. I know Ko's awake. We want to see him!"

Sam looked from the door back to Ko on the bed and lowered his voice to a whisper. "Speak not a word of this, Ko. You and I can discuss it further if you like, when we are away from the others. For now, I'd ask that you push Stranger and her Celestial from your mind, and enjoy time with your sister, Joan, and Leo. The four of you need each other, and you need rest, away from the concerns of Light and Dark for the time being. Can you do that?"

Ko nodded, and with his voice lowered, said, "I won't speak a word about it."

Satisfied with Ko's response, Sam walked to the door and let it swing open.

In rushed Aileen. One bound was followed by another, then a leap into Ko's bed. Aileen landed mostly on Ko, who let out a groan mixed with laughter as he caught her in a hug, shifting his weight to protect his bruises. Aileen hugged Ko back before sitting back on the foot of the bed, looking at her brother with a beaming smile.

"You're up! I thought you'd never wake up!" said Aileen.

"Don't be silly; of course, I'm up. I just like to sleep, that's all," said Ko.

"Ko, the Aphotic, we did it! We saved Leo! Isn't it great? I'm so happy," said Aileen.

"It's amazing, Aileen. I'm so thankful you're safe. You know that I love you, right?"

"Yeah, I know. I love you too," said Aileen.

Ko turned to find Joan leaning against the doorway. Leo stood beside her. Ko and Joan looked at each other, with Joan wearing a sly smile. Ko matched her smile, their looks telling each other, "it's good to see you." Aileen burst again, before Ko or Joan could exchange words.

"Ko! I almost forgot! Did Sam tell you about this?" said Aileen.

Aileen revealed their parents' chain of ultralight.

Ko was entranced by the light his parents had created. It was the first time he had seen it. Sam still stood near the door, leaning against a wall.

"Yes, Sam mentioned it," said Ko.

"Mom and Dad left this for me. It saved us. I wasn't feeling good in the Aphotic, but then I woke up and it was just floating there," said Aileen.

"They loved you very much," said Ko.

"They loved us very much. I miss them. Do you miss them?" said Aileen.

"Yes, I'll always miss them. Somehow, they looked after us in the Aphotic, one last time. Now, we have to look after each other. Will you look after me?" Ko said jokingly.

Aileen smiled. "Of course!"

"What about me?" said Joan.

Joan stepped from the doorway to the edge of the bed and took a seat.

"Who's going to look after me?" said Joan again, tagging along to Ko's joke.

"Ooh! I will!" said Aileen.

"I'm sure you will," said Joan before looking back and motioning for Leo to move from the doorway and closer to the bed.

"Leo, come meet Ko," said Joan.

Aileen beamed at Leo as he approached. Leo was a handsome boy with blond hair and hazel eyes. He had regained most of his color and the vibrance of life since returning from the Aphotic. His skin still shone pale from the extended time he was in the Aphotic, but it shined in a manner akin to Celestials. Ko reached out his hand, Leo did likewise, and they shook.

"It's very good to meet you, Leo," said Ko.

Leo didn't respond; he just smiled softly back at Ko and nodded likewise.

"Leo hasn't spoken since we got back, but he can hear us and understand us. Can't you?" said Joan.

Leo looked at his sister and gently nodded.

"That's okay," said Ko. "My sister tells me that your galaxy is beautiful. I'm very thankful that both you and your galaxy are safe."

"Would you like to see it?" said Joan.

"See it? What do you mean?" said Ko.

Joan motioned to Leo, who responded by gathering swirls of light through the bedroom window, from the Portum Lux sky. Without sound, Leo formed the light into a hologram-like image, floating above the bed, showing a perfect replica of Leo's galaxy. Every aspect of the galaxy was portrayed, with all the colors mixed in and swirled, and each shining mass in its place. The outer rim of the galaxy was splotched with pulsating reds and blues, while the bulk of the galaxy's center was a soft orange light streaked by dark red swirls. Leo's galaxy slowly spun above the room.

Ko was transfixed by the beauty of what floated above him.

"It's amazing," said Ko.

"Yep!" said Aileen.

Leo let the light fade, the image of his galaxy disappearing from the room.

"Thank you for showing me that," said Ko.

"Ko, you know Leo never knew his parents. They left when he was a baby. So, he's kind of like us now, except we got to know our parents," said Aileen.

"That's true, Aileen," said Ko.

"Since you've been asleep, I've been telling Leo about our parents and all the fun things we used to do, but most of all I've been telling Leo about the stories Dad used to tell us. They were always so much fun. I've tried to tell Leo the sea fairy story, but I don't do it like you. Will you tell it to Joan and Leo? I want them to hear it; I think it'll be wonderful," said Aileen.

"What do you think?" Ko asked Joan.

"I'd like to hear it," said Joan.

Ko proceeded to tell the story. About how fairies roamed creation before anything else did, and about the small contingent of fairies who settled in the dunes by the seas. And how the dune fairies sought to become sea fairies and succeeded in doing so with the help of a young boy aided by Light. Leo and Aileen were enthralled with the tale, while Sam and Joan looked on with smiles at the joy of the two young Celestials. A warm feeling came over Ko as he finished telling it.

"See, Leo! Isn't it great! I think the young boy, in the beam of light, was like you and me. Do you want to play with light and create beams, like the boy from the story?" said Aileen.

Leo nodded in agreement to Aileen's proposition, and the Celestials rushed out of the room and into the hall of the Tourlitis lighthouse.

"I think I'd better keep an eye on those two," lamented Sam. "There's no telling where they might end up if that sister of yours creates one of those damn ultralight beams."

Ko and Joan smiled at Sam's agitation as he left the room. Joan reached and held Ko's hand.

"Based on that story, I'd say your parents were truly brilliant," said Joan.

"Yeah, they were brilliant. I didn't know it before. They hid it from us, you know, who we were and whatever they were. Knowing what I know now, I'm not sure if the fairy story they told us makes more, or less, sense," said Ko.

"It makes sense in its own way," said Joan.

"Yeah, I think you're right," said Ko.

Joan and Ko sat in silence for a few seconds, then Joan spoke.

"Ko, what do we do now?"

Ko reflected before responding.

"We enjoy our time."

CPSIA information can be obtained
at www.ICGtesting.com
Printed in the USA
BVHW070554090920
588358BV00003B/190